Don't Shoot the Messenger

J. A. Lenay

Thornfeather Press

CONTENTS

CHAPTER ONE

Rella slides in a side entrance of the Saucy Siren out of habit rather than necessity. As the only tavern on this small secret island deep in the demon pirate Admiral Satrasi's territory, it's more than bustling tonight with multiple ships in port. Even the carrier is just offshore, leaving the tavern packed. Originally the carrier was some government's solution to sustaining long voyages out into the Unbroken Sea. With its own gardens and water purification system, it's a magnificent beast of machine and magic that makes it worth its weight in diamond, but requires a large crew to man. If Rella doesn't want to get shoved, she'll have to make sure she's noticed. The trick to getting everywhere she needs to be for her job as one of the admiral's messengers is either for no one to notice she's even there or for them to think she belongs.

Rella heads up to the second floor to survey the tavern more easily for the captain she's here to find, managing to get a spiked twilsey from a busy barmaid as she does so. Luckily, it's early enough in the night that the majority of the patrons aren't too drunk, and various groups seem to be sticking to who they came with. Since each ship's crew is still somewhat together, Rella's able to go through the rooms, dismissing whole sections of the pub when she recognizes who's staked their claim where.

The *Deliverance* crew is on the first floor. She mentally crosses that area off first, having had to push through a number of them to get to the bar. Rella spots the *Vixen*'s captain easily by her bright red hair and her crew's acrobatics even at the tavern. It takes some minutes of study to recognize the *Gray Mary*'s crew, but she's able to spot Gray Mary herself after her new first mate—a tall demon with even taller horns who's nearly as gray-skinned as she is—moves and stops blocking her from Rella's sight.

Rella follows Peggy, known for her missing leg and other proclivities, to the rest of Captain Red's *New Moon* crew. Rella's glad it's early enough into the night—and the lunar cycle—that none of them is any hairier than usual yet. They're starting to mingle with the crew of the *Brazen Flame*, although she can't tell who their current captain is. All fire demons, they pass around a tiara of rubies they won on their first voyage to whoever their captain that day is. Rella follows one of the whip-thin lads with yellow skin up to the second floor, where he joins some of those she knows the best: all full-time veterans of the carrier.

Unfortunately, that means Rella's searched the majority of the first and second floor without spotting the crew of the *Lux Lady*, let alone Captain Critchley himself. She'd hoped this would be a quick task, but now she'll have to search the add-ons as well.

"Looking for someone, Marlin Rella?" one of the barmaids, Dea, asks as she clears off a table near her.

Rella nods, finishing off the last of her drink and hanging the mug on her belt next to her blade. "New captain who wants to join. Captain Critchley of the *Lux Lady*. You seen 'im?"

Dea straightens at the name. "There's some new folks around back near the tables. Cel'brating some big score, or so they think." She rolls her eyes. "Not that it's encouraged them to share the wealth."

Rella frowns, but she's not surprised. Pirates are either the tightest-fisted misers she's ever met or the biggest spendthrifts this side of the Unbroken Sea, never much in between. It's why half the admiral's edicts are on how to split bounties. "Something must have convinced Captain Jack to vouch for them. Big score might do it for him; he's all about coin."

"Aye," Dea agrees. "They're making friends with the *Serpent* crew that are ashore, so like calls to like."

The *Hungry Serpent* is an odd crew, but their flag of a two-headed serpent fits them to a tee; half of them love nothing more than booze and fighting, and the other half never drink and sent their coin home to family. How they all manage to work next to each other is a mystery.

"Looking for a refill?" Dea's done wiping down the tables near her and is probably itching to get back to the bar.

Rella shakes her head and slips her a bronze coin. She knows Dea wasn't expecting one for such a simple scrap of information, but what was the point of having money these days if she didn't spend it? Besides, a little goodwill can go a long way in her profession.

Dea takes the coin and flashes her a smile before heading off.

Skirting around the central bar, Rella ducks into the nearest of the game halls. Games of cards and dice are being played down below, but every game that needs a table is up top, where it's harder to make off with anything. The Saucy Siren is respected but it's still a pirate tavern: making theft easy would be no different than dangling fresh meat in front of a bear. Everything that can be bolted down is. Maybe even some things that shouldn't be. Honestly, Juanita lucked out when she hired the demon who can climb, since half of the things with any value are up in the rafters.

The billiard tables up here aren't too bad: more for casual fun than intense betting. The room is filled with the sweet-smell of the hookahs rather than the heavy pipe smoke that tends to come with dice players below. From the doorway, Rella spies the *Lux Lady*'s crew. Spotting the gorgon from the *Hungry Serpent* with them seals the deal.

As Rella heads into the room, she adjusts her overcoat, using her sleeve to polish one of the silver buttons that mark her as one of the admiral's messengers. Since Captain Critchley isn't part of the fleet yet, she wants to make sure he can identify her for what she is. All the messengers are given the same dark blue overcoat with the admiral's flag insignia on the breast when they start, but it's up to them to make sure the right people see it and the wrong don't. Rella unbuttons the sturdy navy woolen panel that usually keeps the insignia out of sight.

Picking out Critchley is child's play once she gets closer: newer captains are always the ones with their hats still on at the tavern, sporting shiny new jewelry. He's got a gold bauble with a large pearl on one ear and a dull gray bar through the other. There's a heavy golden compass around his neck that's too bright to be anything except new. Not to mention the way his crew is arranged around him, how they glance his way whenever he raises his voice, that informs the opinion of anyone nearby of his status as a captain. He's well on his way to being properly plastered, so it's a good thing Rella found him before he can't even think straight enough to give her a real answer.

She pushes away her discomfort at drawing and commanding attention to herself. Rella's a Marlin for Satrasi, the Demon Admiral. She lets that knowledge seep into her, remembering her experience, the faith he has in her, and pulls that confidence into her bones. The sound of her boots on the wooden floorboards isn't loud, but it's audible in a way it hadn't been before. She's no taller, but her spine is straighter. Her facial expression is harder, sharper. Subconscious or not, everyone gets out of her way as she closes in on the table.

"Captain Critchley?" Rella asks, enunciating so her voice filters through the noise.

He turns with a looseness to his bones that can only come from strong drink. He peers up the short distance from his seated position to her standing one. "Mayhaps. Who wants to know?"

"Messenger from Admiral Satrasi," Rella says; her name doesn't matter, so she doesn't give it.

His eyes brighten and he straightens. His eyes flick to the admiral's insignia on her coat, but she can see he's unimpressed by her height and physique. After all, she's built for running, not brawling. Despite his position below her, he still tries to angle himself so he's looking down his nose at her. It doesn't work. The overall impression is far more comical than commanding. She stifles a sigh. Rella's used to how people try to puff themselves up, as if they want to show they're important enough for Satrasi's attention. *Amateurs.*

"About time," he says with a smirk. "I was beginning to wonder if coming here was a waste of my time."

Rella resists the urge to raise an eyebrow at that and doesn't bother to respond. He won't need her input to continue.

"We docked yesterday," he tells her, as if that means something. "Jackie-boy said the admiral would talk to us once we got to this little island hideaway, not that we haven't appreciated the time to enjoy ourselves." His smirk widens as he nudges the man to his left and a number of crew members laugh.

"The Admiral received Captain Jack's letter vouching for you as well as your own petition and would like to arrange a meeting in the next few days," Rella says formally when she deduces he's said his piece. She doesn't like the narrowing of his eyes at her words. "He has a certain amount of availability, although he knows you must also be occupied with other matters. Do you have any particular time in mind? Or I could tell you when the admiral is available over the next few days; then you could pick which time and day you'd prefer. Up to you."

"Is it now?" he sneers, leaning over to murmur into another man's ear who snickers in response. "Very well, important men have important things to see to. Of course I am the picture of understanding," he gives a little mock bow from his seat, accentuating the move with a flourish that makes his crew break out into guffaws. "When's the earliest His Majesty can see us?"

Rella frowns. He can play the fool all he wants, but she'll take no disrespect to the admiral, even if he is gin-soaked. "The Admiral can see you in three days' time, at high noon at the earliest. He has two other times free that day and then two the next day."

Captain Critchley's whole demeanor darkens. "Pardon me, girlie, but did you say in three days' time? I must have misheard you. We're not waiting *days* for some attention. You say he's gotten our missives; 'e knows we're here, so now what? He's resting on his laurels? Tryin' to waste our time like it don't mean as much as his?"

Saying that Admiral Satrasi's time *is* more valuable than this green captain's won't get her anywhere. "I only know that he couldn't meet with you until noon in three days' time at the earliest. Is that acceptable to you?"

"No," Critchley scoffs, and his men murmur disgruntledly around him, a chorus of drunk seagulls he keeps around to flatter his own self-importance. "It's not *acceptable*. I'll meet with him tomorrow at noon, thank ya kindly. How do we get up on that massive raft he's got?"

Rella hates when people refuse to listen to the message she's communicating. "Can't get on the carrier until *three* days at noon, at the earliest," she says, as if he's hard of hearing and not hard in the head. "When you pick a time the admiral is available, I shall tell him and he'll arrange to have a boat come to bring you to him."

"You know what? I don't think I like your attitude, you uppity doxy."

Rella finally does raise a brow at him calling her a prostitute, if only because it's such a reach. Even men drunk under tables don't normally assume such given her manner of dress—her well-worn coat, white linen shirt, and plain brown trousers tucked into sturdy brown boots, with no accentuated curves or other flattery, have no overlap with what those employed by the brothels wear. Ignoring those obvious trappings, knowing she comes from the admiral would usually be enough to keep their tongues civil, even if they think they might convince her in bed what they couldn't with their words.

Critchley continues, "Since you can't seem to understand what I'm sayin', why don't you fetch a different messenger with an actual brain rattlin' about in his noggin?"

She's done holding his hand. "No, you're the one who ain't listenin'. Admiral said three days at noon. Or at two after noon or three after that. He was very clear, and that's who I'll be listenin' to, and it's who you'll be listening as well to if you wanna meet with him. So are you meeting with him at one of those times in three days or do you want to hear about the ones four days from now?"

Captain Critchley leans off the back of the bench for the first time and points his bottle at Rella with a glare that might have scared her when she was ten. "And I'm tellin' you I'll meet with him tonight."

"That ain't possible," Rella replies, not caring that he had the audacity to move the timeline up even further—not that it have been any sort of coherent conversation tonight given how sloshed he is. She doesn't know who this rat thinks he is, but *she* has the admiral's ear and he doesn't. Everyone else knows to be polite to the ones carrying their words to the admiral. If he hasn't the sense to work that out, she isn't going to help him. Rella will be sure to tell Satrasi how Critchley's behaving when she gives him the meeting time. She might even pen a letter to Jack herself for sending along a captain with his head so far up his own ass. "The admiral is not available tonight; he made that very clear. I'm not even to bring him your reply until the morning." Normally she wouldn't tell someone that, but she wants to stress to Critchley how impossible his demand truly is.

"I'm afraid that's not gonna happen, wench." Critchley leans forward on the table, setting his bottle down heavily and bracing himself with one splayed hand. "You're gonna take me to that self-important pirate now. He's not any better than the rest of us just because he nabbed a daft oddity of seacraft you can't even raid from. I'm no third-rate cabin boy to be brought to heel by skinny bitches who don't know when to listen instead of yap."

"No," Rella snaps, the last of her patience gone at the insult to Satrasi, let alone his misunderstanding of the carrier's value. "You're a natterin' child, here on the Admiral's generosity, asking for his favor but refusing to wait your turn."

Before her eyes can track it, he's on his feet and a large hand is closing around her throat in an iron grip. Rella's so shocked that he dared to strike her here that she doesn't even react, letting him lift her to the tips of her toes.

His hot, alcoholic breath reeks as he says, "If anyone here is a child, it's you. Playing above your pay amongst those stronger and more important than you. I don't know who lets you get away with that lip, but I'll not stand for it."

Her left hand closes around the fingers he has at her neck, trying to pull them from where they're digging into her skin, cutting off her air when he gives a squeeze to emphasize his point. Fighting to keep any sort of sound from escaping, Rella needs another second to come to terms with the impossible. This lowlife piece of shit dared assault her while on official business from the admiral in his territory.

You're going to regret this.

CHAPTER TWO

Rella's not sure what makes Critchley get out of her face or stop squeezing her throat, since he certainly doesn't let go. Maybe it's the rage in her eyes. More likely, it's the silence that spreads through the room in a wave as everyone else reacts to what he's done.

She tries her best to put her burning lungs and aching throat out of mind as she reaches down to her holster. Murmurs and growls fill the room from their newly attentive audience. Rella cannot believe the nerve of him. The audacity. He's doing this in one of the places she's the safest. She's not afraid, though: that sense of sanctuary isn't shattered.

No, Rella's *furious*.

The silence breaks as scores of flintlocks are drawn and cocked.

"Oi!" one man shouts from nearby. "That's a *Marlin* you're knocking about!"

"Haven't you any sense?" another admonishes.

"Too blitzed to know any better," a woman says, a snicker to her voice.

"His funeral." That one is bored with a hint of teeth. "Wonder if we can scavenge the leftovers."

"They lettin' the brainless in these days?" someone wonders.

"Admiral ain't gonna like this."

And that's why she still feels safe. Critchley might *think* he's got the upper hand, but Rella *knows* she does.

Critchley's drawn his own gun on pure instinct, as have the majority of his crew. Instead of fearful, he's mostly pissed off at the crowd of onlookers. "Can't a man deal with pompous jabbermouths without it becoming every lookie-loos business?"

Rella takes the opportunity to bring his attention back where it belongs. In one smooth motion, she brings her dagger down to rest against his arm. The sensation is undoubtedly light, but the edge is sharp enough to slice through the fabric of his jacket and shirt. He turns his head. The jostling of his arm against the blade scores a line in his skin.

Rella's voice is raspy and harsh from his treatment of her throat, but her job relies on her words, so she makes herself clearly heard. "Let. Me. Go."

His lip curls in a sneer before he sees the silvery gray of the blade, the obsidian and bloodstone hilt, the hungry aura that surrounds the weapon held in Rella's hand. He goes dead white.

"Don't you know all Marlins got demon blades?" an onlooker jeers. "What a scut."

Demon blades are the most dangerous blades to exist. At first glance their grey, mildly lustrous appearance might fool the viewer into believing the curved blades are made of common metal, but all are fashioned from demon bone or claw. Even rarer are those spelled by demon blood magic to never harm their wielder. Sharper than anything and says something about the person who's got one: this person isn't to be trifled with.

While demons are slightly more common in remote areas and, of course, deeper in the Unbroken Sea, they are far outnumbered by humans.

Between the rarity of the material and the rarity of the knowledge needed to make true demon blades, they're highly prized. Rella's was given to her by Satrasi himself, of himself—one of his teeth—and it is bound to her by him personally. Satrasi hones the magical talents he possesses to a wicked degree. The stronger a demon blade is the sharper it is—able to slice through just about anything. Rella's never encountered even another demon blade as sharp as her own.

That understanding flashes through Critchley's mind. She pinpoints the exact moment he realizes she can scythe through muscle and bone. That she could, with no leverage, cut his arm clean off as easily as a hot knife through butter.

He lets her go instantly.

Rella drops down to one knee, even though she hadn't technically been held off her feet, bracing herself with her free hand. She gulps in air even as she keeps her blade pointed at Critchley, who has lost any self-preservation he had gained with her knife to his skin and smirks down at her.

The room is no longer silent, filled with murmurs and tension, no one quite sure what's going to happen next. No one has ever had the audacity—or stupidity—to attack a personal messenger of the admiral on such hallowed ground as the Saucy Siren before.

Rella isn't confused about what's going to happen next. She's going to finish delivering her message tonight, and then deliver the reply in the morning to Satrasi as per her mission. This scum will get what's coming to him then.

With her breathing returning to normal, she starts to push up, only for a mottled brown hand to enter her field of vision. Rella grasps the hand offered by the first mate of the *Hungry Serpent* and allows them to help her up. Once Rella's on her feet, they turn.

"What're ye *doing*?" Takis asks, staring incredulously at Critchley, their hair adding to the effect as multiple snakes join them in staring. Any of the crew from the *Hungry Serpent* who had been mixing with the *Lux Lady*'s crew have now distanced themselves, as if worried the consequences of Critchley's stupidity might be contagious.

"What's it to you?" Critchley snaps.

"This is Admiral territory, and you just attacked a *Marlin*." Takis folds their arms. They glance pointedly at the six silver buttons adorning the outside of Rella's overcoat, visible proof that she's one of the Admiral's Marlins. The rest of her buttons—each one a reward for a significant job she's completed for the admiral—are hidden on the inside, where they won't tempt the greedy. Takis is familiar enough with her to have an idea of just how many buttons she's hiding. "One of the Admiral's best, no less. Can't do that here."

"I can do as I fuckin' please."

"No." Takis leans forward, their expression hard. "Ye can't. Ye ain't one of us, yer a guest. An' we're willing to excuse all manner of fumblin' on account of not knowin' the codes 'round here. This ain't one of 'em. Don't care who ye are or where yer from: ye don't assault a personal messenger of the Admiral."

"The cracknob girlie is fine." Critchley rolls his eyes and picks up his bottle, taking a swig. "If she were doin' her job right, I wouldn't have had to get up close and personal-like."

"You haven't given a proper answer yet." Rella takes this moment to speak, resisting the urge to rub her throat and grimacing inwardly at how rough it still sounds. "When do you wanna meet with the Admiral?"

Critchley swallows another mouthful of gin, confident now that she'll not be retaliating. The lack of menace on her part has reinforced his own belief in either her incompetence or weakness. "And you're still not listening: I'll see him tomorrow. If you don't wanna bring him my answer, that's your problem, not mine."

Rella narrows her eyes at his careless grin and looks over his crew. Those closest to him, and therefore her, are all of the same mind as their captain: sniggering and drinking—unconcerned. They dismiss her or glare at the still on-edge other pirates around them, even if most of them have gone back to their own games now that she's on her feet.

Some of the others, ones who are from the *Lux Lady* but are standing further back, are much warier, even as drunk as they are. They look twitchy, as if they're trying to decide if Critchley or the specter of the admiral is the bigger threat. They seem to think for the moment, it's better to stay by their captain's side, but Rella wouldn't be surprised if they spooked away as easily as minnows in a stream.

Never a good sign when half a captain's crew doesn't trust him. Rella spies the cut-off bits on Critchley's coat that signify he might once have been a navy man, an officer. Those make the worst sort of pirate captain; they always feel eternally cheated and entitled. Resentful. They only manage to stay captain if they've got enough muscle to back them up, which Critchley seems to have... for the moment.

"All right," Rella says. Critchley doesn't bother to hide his surprise at her even-keeled answer. "If that's what your answer is, so be it. Let me know if you change your mind."

She doesn't bother telling him how to contact her if he does, because… well, she knows his type.

He scowls. "I won't."

Rella stares at him for an extra moment before she shrugs. She's delivered her message. Critchley can dig himself as deep as he'd like. It's no skin off her nose. Her gaze flickers over his crew, and they're unsettled by her lack of reaction.

Good.

Rella deliberately turns her back on Captain Critchley. She no longer has any plans to stay here for the evening. Instead, she'll be retiring to her cabin early. She only makes it a few steps before Takis reaches for her elbow.

"Marlin Rella," they say even as she moves away from their hand.

She appreciates their support, but she has a limit on her own patience too, which this night is severely taxing. The thought of her own quarters, of privacy and quiet and of treating her throbbing throat in peace is far more tempting than any siren call.

"What are ye gonna do?"

Rella raises her brows and frowns. "Do? I'm not going to *do* anything."

"He *attacked* you," Takis says. "*Here*. Ye gotta do *something*."

"No," Rella replies, shaking her head only to wince at the strain it puts on her neck, which is aching something fierce. Her throat feels as if there's something stuck in it. "I don't. It's not my code he broke." She doesn't grin, doesn't let anything show on her face, but she has no doubt justice will be served on her behalf. Satisfaction flows through her veins when she says, "Admiral Satrasi will be most displeased."

Takis nods slowly, understanding dawning on their face. "Tomorrow, then."

She brushes off Takis's offer to walk her out. Making her own way to the carrier, she turns her collar up and moves with enough speed and confidence that no one can get a good look at her, let alone her neck. Rella doesn't care who might see or what they might think: she simply doesn't want to have to explain. She can be patient when it comes to Critchley's punishment in the morning, but not now when she just wants to retire for the evening with a soothing tonic.

A weight drops from her shoulders as she crosses the threshold to her cabin and deadbolts the door shut. She carefully lifts her satchel over her head, not wanting to jostle her neck any more than she needs to. She removes her various other accessories, unbuttons her overcoat and waistcoat, and unties her pockets. Clad only in her white shirt and billowy trousers, she opens up her chest of precious medical balms and remedies.

By now, Rella's throat is burning and breathing is harder than makes her comfortable, not to mention the throbbing headache. Thanking the creator of this carrier for their foresight, she pumps water into a basin, drinking some delicately. Soaking some rags in the cold water to drape around her throat, she finds that they do help soothe the ache, although she's careful not to wrap them too tightly.

Rella's used to patching herself up when she can, she's alone too often to be comfortable not knowing all she could on the off chance she's cut off. So even though she has access to the carrier's physician, she'd rather manage on her own. Besides, Rella doesn't want to explain the situation or have to convince someone not to disturb Satrasi, especially when it hurts to speak. He doesn't need his night disturbed after only just returning from a perilous journey.

A selfish part of her does want to disturb him, simply because, between both of their duties and travels, Rella's only seen him twice in the last two months. That greedy part of her craves his attention. But his orders for privacy and her own worry about what that trip might have taken out of him are stronger.

To take her mind off such desires, she's more methodical than usual as she tends to her throat. Referring to her medical book—the most precious book she owns—she carefully measures out ingredients. She's propped up in bed to sleep just as exhaustion threatens to pull her under, glad that since the carrier is anchored tonight, she can use the bed frame for stability rather than her hammock. Weariness rushes over Rella in waves, and she succumbs, content in the knowledge that all will be set right in the morning.

It's deeply comforting to know that someone has her back, is on her side, and perhaps that's why her dreams are full of memories of her first meeting with Satrasi: the first time Rella ever felt that way.

CHAPTER THREE

A few years ago

Rella triple-checked her basket, wanting to make sure she was leaving none of her precious few possessions behind. She didn't have much, so it didn't take long.

She checked her clothing last, making sure her skirt and jacket were as clean as she could make them and her stays were as tight as they could be over her chest. One of the easiest ways to make herself appear younger was by keeping her chest as flat as possible. Folks were less wary and more sympathetic when they forgot how old she was.

Rella'd lived in this town her whole life, so everyone knew the girl orphaned by tragedy, and she wanted them to keep thinking of her that way as long as they would. She wanted to hold onto that goodwill. She wanted them to stay just slightly wary, like that bad luck might be catching. Only trouble could come on the heels of the townspeople realizing she'd grown into a woman of marrying age—or more likely bedding age—two years ago.

Rella had no permanent home, but she had hideaways she frequented: an overhang by the river, Old Man Mills's outlying barns, the ruins of the road lookout. Today, she headed for the cave on the outskirts of town.

Away from the river proper, it was far less frequented and, with its own freshwater pool fed by some underground river offshoot, made for a good respite from the sun and its heat.

Unfortunately, the cave wasn't a hideout she could stay in long term: too cold in the winter and very insecure, not to mention that her back ached from sleeping on stone for too long. Still, it would be a wonderful escape for a few days, giving her time to think and take stock of what she had. She liked to give the town a break from her presence so no resentment or annoyance started to fester. It was a fine line to walk between "helpful, pitiable orphan" and "troublesome, layabout beggar."

She ducked off the road and headed down to the cave, eyes sharp for any signs someone else might have thought it a good place to camp out. Right by the entrance, she spotted some odd tracks in the dirt, almost like snakes. Her eyes narrowed: there weren't any animals of that sort around here, and she was fairly certain the forest demon that roamed these woods preferred to appear either deer-like or wolf-like rather than snake-like. She certainly had no desire to run into them. Wary, she waited in the shadows, listening and watching for any sign someone else might already be in her refuge.

Rella's pulse raced as she crouched in the bushes, but when nothing happened, discomfort from sticks digging into her knees and sweat from the humidity dripping down her back were enough to override her paranoia. Rella crept into the cave, ready to flee if even a single rock was out of place. Slowly her hackles lowered, as the cave appeared as it always had been and no sound—not even of someone sleeping—reached her ears.

All she found was a rusted, bent belt buckle that had to have been here for weeks. Maybe a traveler had taken advantage of the cave rather than paid for a night at the inn and this was all they'd left behind. It had happened before.

Finally secure in the knowledge she was alone, Rella left her jacket and her basket in an alcove invisible from the main cave and headed for the pool.

Illuminated by faint rays of sunlight filtering into the dark, the pool's surface was still, barely reflection the white stalactites above. The water went all the way to the far wall of the cave and reached deeper under the rock than she could ever swim. Every few years, the young and the brash dared each other to see if they could find the secret room legend said held treasure if only someone could swim far enough, but no one ever had. Rella was fairly certain the water never hit the air again. She was always grateful when the others forgot about the cave once more.

Rella leaned down, cupping some of the cool, clear water and slurping, only for a glint to catch her attention. Was there something reflective in the water? She narrowed her eyes and reached in, holding the edge of the pool with one hand as she plunged the other down. There was a narrow shelf around the edge of the pool and the water went past her elbow before her hand closed around something long and metallic, but pliable too. She frowned as she sat on her heels next to the pool to study her prize.

It was almost like a braid of silver, not quite a chain. A lanyard of some sort? But why make one out of silver? Awfully pricey for a bit of flash. It didn't appear to be a necklace or bracelet: too thick for that and the wrong length. How would one even wear this? Had this been in the depths of the pool all these years? Wouldn't the silver have been more tarnished? She had certainly never seen it before.

"Did you find my aiguillette? Thought I'd lost it," an echo-y, but deep, voice made Rella's head whip up. How could she have missed someone else being here?

Rella found herself staring across the pool to the far wall of the cave. Glowing red eyes with black pupils stared back at her from just over the water's surface. They blinked. All four of them. Two smaller eyes without any pupils at all were situated off the outer corners of their primary eyes.

Demon, her mind supplied.

The eyes moved up, getting higher even though the water didn't so much as ripple at the demon's movement. They moved closer too, but she couldn't find the energy to get up. To flee. She was fairly certain it wouldn't matter if she had. Demons were notoriously fast and strong. If this one wanted to catch her, she was already caught.

Some light finally illuminated more of them as they moved. Slick, gray skin and scattered clusters of dull red scales reflected only some of that light. The brief glimpse of the demon's facial expression indicated they were amused more than anything, which she supposed was better than hungry.

"How about you hand that back over to me, hm?" he asked, coming to a halt about two yards from her. His eyes darted to where she had the silver braid clutched to her chest.

Silver was worth something: even the town blacksmith would be able to give her good coin for it, not to mention a silversmith at the port. Even still, Rella didn't hesitate in tossing it to him. Not only did it sound like it had been his to start with, and she was no thief, but no bit of flash or coin was worth her life.

An arm reached to catch it with ease, although... Rella frowned. There was a frilled fin coming from his forearm, but it was dull and limp, almost fragile. While he ran his fingers over the silver, she noticed that all of his skin—or was it scales on a sea demon?—was similarly dull and pale. Were they actually gray? Or some other color that had become washed out?

"My thanks," he said. He sounded sincere enough, despite his amusement, that her eyes snapped back to his strange ones. He appeared to be studying her with interest. Her skin prickled with nerves. Rella preferred to remain beneath most people's notice and this demon was no exception. Still, what if fleeing made him want to chase? What would he do when, not if, he caught her?

She couldn't meet his gaze for long without losing her sense of where she was. Her heart pounded, and in an attempt to get it to calm down, Rella let her eyes trail over him rather than continuing to meet his unnerving gaze. Noticing he wasn't wearing a stitch of clothing didn't help.

Eyes narrowed Rella focused on a silent sort of movement in the water around him. It was closest to the faint scar running down the middle of his chest, which moved as if he was breathing heavily. However, nothing about his voice suggested he was out of breath. Odd. She had to stop herself from leaning closer for a better look, instead squinting to try to make out a glint of... teeth?

All of a sudden the image solidified to her. He didn't have a scar down his front: it was a mouth with long, almost metal-looking teeth in it, opening and closing as it took in water. Rella froze, all of her muscles going tight at the sight. Goosebumps spread to cover her skin.

"No need to be so nervous," he said, definitely entertained by her fear. "You're hardly more than a morsel."

A shiver went down her spine at his words, even though she believed he could eat far more than just her and not be full. Each second that passed without him attacking helped ease only a few of her nerves.

When next she refocused on his face, he was leaning closer, his own eyes narrowed at her. "Do you speak at all, little bite?"

Rella flushed. "When the situation calls for it."

He laughed at that, revealing pointy, bright white teeth. "Well said. What brings you to this lovely cave? I've been here for days with no visitors."

"I wouldn't think you would," she said, adjusting her seat, interested in what he might reveal in spite of herself. "No one really comes here except children trying to see how far they can swim." Rella nodded toward where the pool went under the rock wall. "Too out of the way for most townsfolk."

"So there is a town nearby," he muttered.

Rella frowned. "What are you doing out here, if you don't even know about the town?"

His smirk returned at her question. "Some folks managed to get the jump on me, intent on cashing in a bounty from the Governor, if their chatter is to be believed."

Rella didn't need to hear the rest. He must be some sort of bandit, or more likely a pirate, given his nature. In general, the governor of her province didn't have an outstanding warrant for demons, so this one had to have done something special to earn a bounty substantial enough to warrant a group going after him.

Pursing her lips, she gave him another sweeping look as she thought on his story. Now fully adjusted to the low light, her eyes raked over his form, taking in everything from his small movements to the exact color of his scales. There it was: a gash on his shoulder Rella hadn't noticed but which she now saw was fresh. Something else on the same side of his torso also looked damaged, even through the refraction of the water.

"I assure you, they came out of the encounter far worse." His voice had more of a hiss to it this time. It wasn't said defensively, instead he said it as though he didn't want her getting any bright ideas.

As if Rella thought herself able to take this demon on; even if he'd been missing the arm entirely he'd overpower her in a heartbeat. She survived by not being noticed, and by making herself useful enough to outweigh any burden she might cause, not by picking fights with people able to kill her as easily as she would a bug.

"You're stuck, though, aren't you?" Rella asked, sensing the truth.

He raised his brows at that, leaning against a stalagmite that reached up from down below. "Is that so?"

But she knew she was right. Sea demons needed the sea, and this pool was fresh water. The fight he'd been in might justify a brief rest to recover, but despite being here for a few days, he'd not moved on. Beyond that, he looked faded, or maybe even swollen? It was so hard to tell, but something wasn't right. This water might be better than no water, especially after however long he'd been captured for, but it was *not* the sea.

"Sea's more than three days' ride from here," Rella said, answering what she hoped was his real question. "By road. Can't get around the mountain on foot any faster than going through."

He hummed thoughtfully, the sound resonating through the air and water. "I see."

Rella decided to chance moving. Leaning to the right, she took the waterskin she had and filled it up before leaning over to drink directly from the pond itself.

"Bold little creature, aren't you?" he commented.

Rella's eyes moved to meet his once more. She was good at reading what people thought of her, and while no one had ever called her 'bold' before, she could tell he—at least—didn't think it a bad thing. If anything, he was entertained—or possibly even impressed by her actions. No one had ever been impressed by Rella before.

He continued, "I think I might be offended if you're over your fear so quickly."

Rella tilted her head to the side as she considered his words. "You already said you'd no plans to eat me, and if you wanted to, I doubt this distance"—she motioned between them—"would cause that to go any different. And I'm thirsty."

He chuckled, the sound bouncing around the cave. He hadn't made any demands, acted aggressively toward her, or threatened her. Rella's long-honed instincts about people cautiously rated him as not a threat. Dangerous because of what he was and that he might be in a desperate situation, but with no intention of causing harm at the moment. That was the most Rella generally hoped for.

He gestured at the water and said, "Far be it for me to stop you, little bite."

Rella blinked once at him before taking another sip, slurping even louder than before, not sure what about him was bringing about this cheeky side of her. Maybe it was that he was the first person in a while who wasn't inclined to take advantage of her right up until they kicked her out.

After drinking her fill, she looked up to see he had slipped below the water's surface again. Rella worked on patching her clothes in the light by the cave mouth. While she would usually take her time to relax and enjoy the lack of back-breaking farm labor in the cool cave, the demon lurking in the water nearby drove her to use the chore as an excuse to avoid him.

What had happened to him? Were all demons this compelling? The demon in the forest near the town certainly wasn't the beguiling type. Maybe sea-demons were different; the rumors certainly said so, but Rella didn't put much stock in those. He seemed intelligent enough, if intimidating. Would his enemies find him here? She could barely wrap her mind around one such oddity in her sleepy town; any more excitement seemed impossible. Maybe she should leave the cave, after all.

After her mending was done, Rella resettled to eat. She was chewing on bread when the demon resurfaced. He didn't speak, but he did watch her silently, as if he was weighing his next few words with care. She glanced down at the food she had to last her the next few days. She mentally tallied up how long her supplies would last if she had to feed him too; even if she managed to gather some berries they likely wouldn't last long. It was hard to gauge height with him in the water, but he'd called her a morsel, so she figured his appetite must be large.

"No need to fret, little bite," he said, voice sounding even wetter than before, which Rella hadn't thought possible. "I've no need to pilfer your scraps. There's food enough for me in the water."

Rella blinked and then leaned forward to ask, "Is there? Never seen any fish in the pool. There are only rumors of treasure so deep none can reach it."

He smirked. "No treasure that I've seen, but there are some other pools—close but not connected—that I can move between."

Rella listened to him talk of his exploration, content to hear strange tales in his even stranger voice. She felt the weight of his red, red gaze every time she asked a question. She wondered if he was mesmerizing her—she had heard tell of sirens who could do that—but why would he bother?

When he was done talking about the caves and she was done eating, he swam closer and asked about the town. This was more the type of talking Rella had expected, though he needn't try to hypnotize her to get it.

It was strange how comfortable Rella felt with him. She had never even met a demon or a pirate before, but maybe that was part of it. Maybe it was that she knew how strong he was and so there was no point in worrying about it. Maybe it was that it was nice to be seen and not worry about the consequences. He was so far beyond this small town and its small-minded people. Maybe it was just that he was giving Rella a taste of the world beyond this place that appeared more enticing by the day.

Leaning against the wall of the cave with her arms wrapped around her knees, Rella found her eyes constantly tracing his inhuman features. His eyes, the wild tentacles he had in place of hair, each new cluster of red scales that her eyes could find—every bit of him captivated her: so unusual and beautiful. Even so, the more time she spent watching him, talking with him, the more she felt a worry grow in the back of her mind.

Worry for him.

Because he was not well. The unnatural color of his skin, the strange—almost swollen—puffiness to his form, the way he was almost squishy... it all concerned her. Even the way that strange mouth continued to heave in his chest couldn't be right. A physician only visited her town once a week, if they were lucky. Rella doubted he knew anything about demon physiology or any interest in learning it, given the way most around here felt about demons. Not to mention sea demons were fundamentally different from the other sort. Maybe someone at a port might be able to help, but she didn't think he could leave this pool. Unless that was what was making him sick? But if it were, why was he still here?

"Little bite?"

Rella blinked, startled from her thoughts.

"I've a proposition for you."

"What sort of proposition?" Even though she'd previously liked the lack of expectations, she knew as well as anyone: when one needed help, politeness or pride had no business being in the picture.

"You were right earlier," he admitted with a disgruntled frown, though she was fairly certain it was only due to the situation he found himself in. "I was held out of water for entirely too long. This fresh water is barely any better. If you can get word to my crew, or even just fetch me some supplies to help me gather enough strength to leave this hole, I'll reward you handsomely."

Rella assumed his crew was at the port. It was a minimum six-day commitment to go there and back—regardless of her ability to find said crew. That was a lot to ask. As for provisions...

"What sort of supplies?" Rella had heard all sorts of tales about exotic ingredients only found in shady back alleys of large cities, from far-off remote places, or from rare creatures. Half of them were items that had to be taken with force and none were in her price range of no coin at all.

"Salt," he said. "Sea salt preferably, but any salt will do. Ten pounds of it at least."

Such a basic ingredient surprised her, especially given his demonic nature, before she remembered that sea demons didn't have the same weaknesses as other demons. It was why there were so many more of them and why the sea was such a dangerous place. The main limitation they had was that plenty couldn't leave the sea that gave them such strength. While there was certainly salt in the village, no one would sell her that much—not with the monopoly the Governor had. Rella didn't have the money for it regardless. Trying to take some from everyone would be too risky as well.

"I'd have to go to the port for that," she said, not bothering to explain why she couldn't get salt here. "I'd need money and food to get me there, at least," she pointed out.

He nodded, not at all thrown off by her request. "I'll tell you where the wreckage from my fight with my captors is. They had wagons and other supplies. Since they were avoiding towns, I bet no one else has found it yet."

"How do you know I won't just take that salvage and leave you here?"

"I don't," he said bluntly. "Beyond that, I assure you I can offer far more than such meager scraps... if you take my deal."

"What if I go through all this trouble and get back to find you dead or gone?"

"That's a risk you'll have to take," he conceded.

Rella appreciated how upfront he was. "I don't work with people I don't know," Rella said, more out of habit than expecting anything in return.

"Name's Satrasi," he replied easily. "We've already been talking. What more do you want to know?"

Satrasi. She repeated his name to herself. She didn't need to know anything more about him, not really. She had already made up her mind. "Mine's Rella. Where's the wreck?"

Satrasi smiled.

Chapter Four

The wreckage from Satrasi's kidnappers' carriage and wagon had been easier to find than Rella had feared. Ignoring the scattered bones of what likely had been his captors, and anything too big to carry by herself, Rella had still found items she could use and sell. The coin she'd kept to herself, the jewelry she'd sold, leaving her with more coin than she'd ever in her entire life. It had been more than enough to pay a family to take her to the port without exchanging work for the ride, as she had in the past, and still have plenty left over to buy Satrasi's salt—something she planned to do right before she returned to Satrasi.

And so, three days later, Rella hid in the shadows of the port market-place as she considered how best to find Satrasi's crew.

Satrasi's ship wasn't docked in the port itself to avoid seizure, but some of his crew should be there, getting supplies and enjoying what entertain-ments the port had to offer. He'd given her descriptions and matching names for a handful of them. Crucially, he'd also drawn his flag in the dirt. Apparently, some of the crew would have that insignia as tattoos or on their clothes.

Rella started near the docks, trying to find taverns that had more than just locals or regular sailors in them, but that weren't obviously dangerous. She knew she'd have to get to those eventually, but she was in no rush.

The fourth tavern was where she found her first demon, so she decided to linger on this row of bars more than the others. She fought through smoke and pressing bodies to look for those she sought without drawing attention to herself and ended up in the next tavern over almost without realizing.

She had nearly given up on this side of the street when she spotted the best candidate she'd seen so far. A demon woman was holding court at a table. Her three thick red tendrils with long black streaks down them for hair, gray skin with green scales spread more like freckles, and green eyes, solid with a black pupil like Satrasi, matched the description of one of Satrasi's crew: his navigator, Dietha. She was drinking enough to enjoy herself but not enough to end up under the table.

As the demon lifted her drink to her lips, Rella spotted it. Her hair-tendrils moved to reveal a red arm band tied around her upper arm, with an insignia that matched the one Satrasi had sketched. One of the others she was with, a plain man with brown hair, had what might be a tattoo of the same on his arm, but it was partially hidden under his shirt and muddled by the other tattoos around it.

Rella found a spot to linger nearby and nursed her own flagon of cider. They might be less of a threat when a little more wobbly on their feet, but she didn't want them incoherent either.

The man was a good storyteller, and Dietha, if that was who she was, added enough to the tales to deepen and ground them. They worked well together, earning themselves drinks without shelling out their own coin, and Rella found herself listening just to listen. While she was smart enough to know these stories had a bit of gloss to them, it seemed like an exciting life: the travel and the crew and the Unbroken Sea.

The others nearby clearly agreed many of them starry-eyed as they listened. Someone teased a man perhaps even a year or two younger than Rella for buying into their romanticized tales, and the crowd laughed.

"Do you always pull such a crowd of people with nothing but cotton between their ears?" an older woman joked. She'd been listening with interest, but there were no rose-colored lenses over her eyes.

"Ye get all sorts who want to hear fearsome stories or even try their luck stealing from pirates," the demon said almost lazily as she elbowed someone pressed too close to her. They blanched and hurried away, to the amusement of the crowd. "'Course, there are always some who want summat more mysterious. Ain't that right, lass?" She turned to Rella. Rella's eyes widened as the demon smirked. "Didya think I hadn't noticed ye lurking in the shadows? Watchin' us? Or 'ave ye just never seen a demon afore?"

"I've seen a demon before," Rella replied, walking closer. She worked hard to seem nonchalant, ignoring the few still listening even when story-time was over. "More fearsome than you, even though he were in rough shape."

"That so? Brave little thing, aren't ya?" The demon's look was appraising as she leaned back in her chair, her eyes half-lidded. "Must have been to survive such a run-in and be here to tell of it."

The man with her scoffed. "Lyin', more like it."

These were not people to show any weakness in front of. Rella shrugged. "Believe what you like."

"If it ain't curiosity that's got yer eye on us, what has?" the demon asked, hand absently traveling over the green spiky frills on her forearm.

"Lookin' for someone," Rella replied, trying to match the pirate's lazy confidence as well as she could. People liked folks who were similar to them, as long as it wasn't an obvious enough imitation to come across as insulting. It made them feel safer, like they knew her and what she wanted. It made her seem predictable. "He ships out with a crew. Tryin' to figure if it's yers."

"Oh, are ye now?" The demon was more interested at that. "Ye manage to get a name afore he scampered out of yer bed?"

"I did," Rella said, not bothering to address the implication she'd slept with the person she was looking for, since at least it meant they didn't think she was a child. "Wicklow, he's called."

Recognition sparked in them, but so did an equal amount of skepticism.

"See?" the man said with a laugh and a slap of his knee. "A liar. Didn't I tell ya?"

"We might know a Wicklow; plenty around," the demon allowed before shaking her head. "But I doubt it's the same one."

"Why's that?" Rella was feeling more confident now that they'd admitted to knowing a Wicklow.

"'Cause he likes his women able to snap him in two," the man said. "Not likely to fall over if he so much as breathes on 'em."

"Ain't after him as a bedmate." Rella made a mental note to perhaps check a certain type of brothel after this if they stonewalled her. "Gotta message for 'im."

"That so?" The demon raised an eyebrow. "From who?"

"His captain, a'course," Rella said, trying not to dwell on how their attention instantly sharpened on her when she was trying so hard to remain nonchalant. "Who else would be lookin' for him? They got split up, yeah? Well, I found the captain."

The demon's eyes narrowed as she pushed away her mug. "This demon ye met. What sort was he?"

Rella was glad the demon had picked up on that. "Sea demon, red eyes, more teeth than ye'd expect in more places than ye would imagine." Her eyes deliberately darted to the armband the demon had tied around her bicep with Satrasi's insignia on it.

"Got anything to prove yer not just tellin' tales?"

Rella swallowed before risking to ask, "Yer name Dietha?"

A slow grin spread across Dietha's face, revealing bright, white teeth, baring the two blank spots where a couple were missing. "Mayhap we do have summat to talk about after all."

She ushered Rella to a smaller side room for a more private conversation. Rella followed Dietha in, trying not to make the tension screaming through her body obvious. She wasn't sure if she succeeded, but they let her have the seat closest to the now closed door. Dietha, the brown-haired human crewman, and a third crew member—a rare half-demon, judging by their blend of human and demon features—took up seats on the other side of the table, fresh drinks in hand.

"Now, what's this tell about Wicklow's captain and messages? They got split, ye say?"

Rella frowned, able to tell Dietha was still asking to see what her story was for the sake of it, rather than because she believed her. "Yeah, Satrasi said some mercenaries got the drop on them on the other side of the port." Their attention sharpened on Rella at Satrasi's name. "Kept 'im in a cage after hightailing away with him. Left Wicklow and another alive when they ran, or at least that's how it'd seemed to 'im."

The crew members exchanged looks Rella couldn't read.

The man said, slowly, "It 'as been longer than usual. They was due back two days ago."

"They've been late before," the half-demon said. Rella thought they might be a he from the voice, but it was hard to tell with the heavily striped features and the lack of hair.

"You didn't even know they were in trouble?" Rella couldn't help but ask incredulously.

The half-demon scowled, offended, but the man was still skeptical. Dietha simply continued to assess her.

"Ain't got tabs on them," the man said. "No way to chat while they meet with some of our more elusive contacts."

"Wouldn't Wicklow be back by now, to get yer help, after running into trouble?" Rella persisted, not even thinking about how that might make them doubt her story.

Dietha snorted, and the half-demon's scowl grew even more pronounced. "That fool takes his position as first mate too seriously. Probably thought he could get the Admiral back quicker and without us having to fret. Lad's only got two ways of being: handle everythin' himself, or drunken despair."

"That seems like a problem in a first mate."

"You'd think so." Dietha laughed. "Problem is, more than half the time he handles things better than anyone else."

"Admiral lets him get away with too much shit," the half-demon spit.

"Admiral prefers loyalty and brains, and that's ninety percent of what Wicklow is," Dietha countered.

Scoffing, the half-demon said, "Yeah, well, the rest is hysterics. Not worth it to my mind."

"Not *your* mind that matters, lad," Dietha said plainly before turning back to Rella. "Now, you claim to have found the Admiral in some hidey-hole. Summat with water, I presume?"

"Yeah," Rella confirmed, "but it's fresh, so even if I couldn't find you lot, he said to bring him salt. Said it would help."

"Aye, it would," Dietha said with a slow nod. "He hurt?"

Rella shrugged. "Not bleedin' out, if that's what yer asking. More sick from the water than anything, I think. I didn't get too close a look."

"Right." Dietha tapped her fingers on the table, thinking.

"Yer not taking this girl seriously, are ya, Dietha?" The half-demon was incredulous. "She's just tellin' tales."

"To what end, Hayleth?"

"Good point," the man said as he turned to Rella. "What's in it for you, pipsqueak? Why run hither and yon for a trapped demon pirate ye don't know?"

"He paid me," Rella said, knowing they didn't care about her hopes on moving to the port. Or even how she wanted to help Satrasi because he was trapped and withering in a hole. How he'd treated her fairly, spoken to her honestly. Rella respected him, and that was rare in her life. And he *had* paid her—not like that wasn't important. "Said he'll give me more if I tell the right people, bring the salt. Can't do that if he's dead. And I got plans that don't begin in my backwater town, let alone end there. Best way to get out I've had fall into my lap. Not gonna let it slip through my fingers."

"We'll need to tell the rest of the crew, but I think this is worth looking into." Dietha glared at Hayleth when he made to protest once more.

He shut his mouth with a grumble.

"She knows too much not to," she said to him before turning back to Rella. "We ain't bringin' no riches with us when we come," she warned. "Admiral said he'd pay ye, so that's who'll do it, yeah?"

"Yeah," Rella replied because fair was fair. She'd expected nothing more. "Town's Millriver, up the east road, through the mountains, about three days' ride, depending. Inn's called the 'Duck and Duchess' and I'll show you where from there."

"Not gonna draw us a little map right to the Admiral?" Hayleth asked, his grin mocking.

"Only supposed to tell Wicklow more than that." Rella's reply was flat. She didn't want it to be obvious how intimidated she was, even though she knew any one of them could kill her if they wanted to.

"Smart girl," the man said.

"Smart Admiral," Hayleth corrected. "What if she told the wrong folk? Miracle she got us."

Rella didn't bother working up any offense at his attributing what she'd done to luck rather than skill. It was what most folks did. It was part of what kept her under anyone's notice—and more importantly, alive.

Dietha hummed thoughtfully before waving in dismissal. "Until then, little messenger."

From what the trio said, Wicklow hadn't been heard from anymore than Satrasi had, which left the question of where he was and what he'd been doing since he'd not alerted the rest of their crew. Dietha and the other two seemed convinced he was trying to find Satrasi on his own, which sounded ridiculous to Rella. They did appear to be certain he wasn't in the port. Which left Rella wondering—where to look?

Satrasi hadn't mentioned anywhere else besides this port, and she was no tracker to figure out where Wicklow had been separated from Satrasi and his kidnappers with any degree of accuracy. In the end, since all she knew was that they'd moved from the other side of the port toward Millriver, looking for him on her way back to Satrasi was all she could come up with. If she took a longer, more circuitous route she could check some other local taverns and inns along the way.

When Rella bought the salt before leaving the port, she had to resist the urge to hold onto the coins, never having had so much and not liking losing the security they gave her. But she'd given Satrasi her word and she stuck by it. At least she was fairly certain she got a good price: the man wasn't angry when she left, but he wasn't as cheery as he had been with the man before her.

At each tavern and inn Rella scouted on her journey, she got her hopes up and was disappointed, as there was no sign of someone matching Wicklow's description in any of them.

Then, at one of the last towns, a day's walk from Millriver, she found him. She'd offered to help with the dinner chores at the inn in exchange for staying in their stables—she couldn't justify paying the amount they charged for a proper room. As she was hammering out the details, she scanned the main room out of habit more than hope and spotted a man who matched Satrasi's description. Or so she thought. It was rather hard to tell.

He was down to his shirt and breeches, face half in his mug of ale, but his hair was the right color as was his build. When one of the barmaids saw her looking, she said he'd been there for a few nights, disappearing each day and then drinking heavily each night. Unfortunately, not pickpocketable despite his inebriation. He had enough to be paying his tab as he went. The barmaid wished he wasn't taking up one of their largest tables by himself and occasionally singing sad ballads off-key.

After watching him discreetly for a while, Rella eventually spotted a tattoo on the back of his hand that was close enough to the skull with tendrils for hair and four eyes that Satrasi sketched for her to decide he was worth the risk of approaching.

"Are you Wicklow?" Rella asked cautiously, not sure how he would act as a drunk but recognizing that subtlety was not likely to work at this point.

He didn't pick up his head, only moaned and said, "Does it even matter anymore?"

Dramatic and sad. That was what the crew at the port had said.

"It does, because I've got a message for Wicklow."

He turned his head to the side to blink blearily at her. "What more bad news could they bestow on poor Wicklow?" he lamented. "Has he not been brought low enough?"

Lovely, talking about himself in the third person. Never a good sign. Would he even remember this conversation come morning? But she couldn't let that doubt seep into her voice; he'd surely take it as a cue to sink deeper into his cups. "So you are Wicklow? Good. Satrasi said—"

He bolted upright at the name fast enough that Rella jerked her head back. Ought he be able to spring up that fast, as full of ale as he was?

"The Admiral?" Then his expression fell, and he gestured with his whole arm. "Spare me your lies! Satrasi got taken, and I've lost the trail. It's been days and days. I sent Millie back to the ship, but she's not back yet either, but she was hurt, you see? So it's just me, and they went through streams and over rocks, and I've no notion of where they could be on this side of the mountain. My captain, in their heartless clutches."

Dear gods, had this man once been in a theater troupe? She had't heard such bellyaching since she'd had to watch Ginnie's youngest while she was off visiting her gran. "Yes, well, he got free on his own, only now he's stuck 'cause he can't get to the sea."

"You've seen him?" Wicklow lunged for her, but stopped inches from her only to clutch at the back of a chair. "Spoken to him?"

At least he was hearing her. "Yes, stumbled upon him in a cave."

"A cave?" He wrinkled his nose. "Why would he be in a cave?"

"Because it was the closest water he could find," Rella explained slowly as he blinked at her. "Even if it's not the sea. There's a pool in it."

"How wise of him," Wicklow said, nodding vigorously and then grasping at his head. "How unwise of me."

Rella winced and surveyed the tavern. The innkeeper seemed glad she was dealing with this mess, and so she was able to get some bread into Wicklow's hand relatively quickly. "Mayhap it's time for a bite of food, yeah?" Rella asked.

Wicklow stared at the bread before looking at her.

"Or some water?" she tried next.

"But what of Admiral Satrasi?" he asked around a mouthful of bread. Even as he accepted the tin cup of water Rella pressed into his hand, Wicklow protested, "We should make haste to him."

"I'm not sure you can make haste in your state," she pointed out.

He swallowed all the water and straightened, his expression losing some of its waver. "Nonsense," he said brusquely, the most coherent he'd sounded since she'd run into him. "A bit of ale isn't going to delay me. He can't be in fresh water for very long, you see."

"Yes, I know,"Rella replied, not trusting the veneer of sobriety he was trying to put on. "He bid me to bring him salt."

"Good, good." Wicklow was smart enough not to nod along with his agreement this time. "That certainly should help. You know where he is? Is it nearby?"

"Yes," she said tentatively. This was the only person Satrasi had said to trust with the actual details of where he was, and, for the first time, she questioned the validity of his decision. "Only a day's walk."

"Splendid. Let's go." He stood up, took one step forward, and promptly fell over.

Rella stared down at him and sighed. "Right."

CHAPTER FIVE

When morning came, Wicklow was still out cold. Rella wasn't surprised, considering that the stablehand had had to carry him up to his room last night, but on the bright side, he'd stayed put. Should she wait for him to wake up?

No. Satrasi needed the salt, and she'd already spent enough time away from him. Besides, once she got the salt to Satrasi, she could come back for Wicklow.

Decision made, she scribbled a deliberately minimalist map on a scrap of paper and tucked it into his pants. As much as she didn't like rifling through Wicklow's pockets, she liked the thought of someone else finding the map even less. She just hoped Wicklow could follow the labelless map in his hungover state.

At least for this last leg of the journey, she could stop worrying about Wicklow and head directly for the cave.

When Rella got to the cave, it was as silent as ever. Her footsteps and the sound of her panting breath—hot and fast from her trek through the woods with the heavy bags of salt—echoed loudly.

Dropping the bags to the ground with a dull thud, she headed directly for the pool. She fell to her knees, sticking her face into the water to drink.

By the time she'd had enough to satisfy her thirst and for her breathing to level off, a spike of concern jabbed insistently at her.

Satrasi hadn't surfaced.

Instead, there was only stillness. "Satrasi?" Rella asked, her voice echoing in the cave.

The longer he didn't answer, the more her concern grew. Was Satrasi gone? Should she just heave one of the bags of salt into the pool? Would that make the pool undrinkable? Would that waste the salt? Did she have enough? Was it even worth bothering with if he was gone, or too far gone for it to do any good? Maybe he'd ventured deeper into the cave and couldn't tell she was here. But shouldn't he be close by awaiting her return?

In the end, Rella opened a bag, took a handful of salt, and threw it as far out into the pool as she could. A chunk of it stuck together and made a muted splash as it sank deeper into the water, but the rest dispersed over a wider area than she'd expected. The light illuminated the specks in the air until they hit the surface of the water and dissolved.

And then she waited.

And waited.

Rella waited long enough to feel foolish, long enough that worry shivered down her spine. She started to think about what to do next before a flicker of movement caught her eye. She breathed out in relief as Satrasi's head breached the surface, but the relief was fleeting.

Satrasi's eyes were still red, but they weren't glowing like they should. His skin stretched over his muscles—rough, puffy, and bloated. The tentacles growing from his head stuck out strangely, seeming less alive than they had before. He looked exhausted. That lessened, though, when he spotted Rella.

Her heart picked up speed at the gratitude and hope in his eyes because of *her*.

Faster than she expected given his current condition, he swam right up to the lip of the pool. "Little bite," he said, his voice muffled and wet, like his tongue was swollen and he had to talk around it. "You came back."

"'Course I did. Got the salt and found some of your people."

Rella tilted the opened bag toward him, and he wasted no time in reaching for some salt. He pulled one handful down into the water, no doubt toward that second mouth, and shoved another fistful into his more human mouth.

Eyeing the limp, fragile, and nearly colorless fins on his forearms with dismay, Rella wondered if there was any other way to help.

It wasn't until he'd taken at least half the first bag that he looked beyond her. "Where...?"

"Navigator Dietha wanted to get more crew and verify my story. First Mate Wicklow I found yesterday, drunk practically under the table." Rella couldn't keep her disapproval to herself. "Gave him the message, though I'm not sure how much he'll remember."

Satrasi blinked at her, truly focused on her for the first time since she'd returned. Maybe it was just wishful thinking that the salt could be helping so quickly, but some of the glow appeared to leak back into his eyes. "You found both of those two?"

"Yes," Rella replied, unsure in the face of his surprise but not wanting to show it. "Dietha was at a tavern in the port a few days ago. She knew it was taking you longer than expected to come back, but not that anything had happened to you because no one who'd gone with you had returned. Wicklow was in a tavern in Halletburg, having tracked you that far, but he'd lost the trail there. I figured I could go back for him once I got you the salt."

Satrasi stared at Rella, going longer without blinking than he should. Usually that would make her uncomfortable, but she felt entranced by his gaze, finding new flecks of black and gold amongst the red of his eyes. He leaned closer, reaching out to catch her chin between his thumb and forefinger. His touch was wet and cold, and his skin had more give than she expected for all his obvious strength.

Rella waited, barely breathing, for him to say something, for his verdict on how she'd performed on the mission he'd entrusted to her.

"Impressive, little bite," Satrasi murmured; she could almost feel his voice like she felt his breath against her lips. "Very impressive." He eased back slowly, and Rella felt an inexplicable pang of loss at the distance. "I'd only hoped you might find one, and even that seemed like a long shot. I'll not underestimate you again."

Her eyes were still locked on his, and Rella didn't want to look away. She didn't want to leave this bubble, this moment frozen in time outside of the rest of the world where someone intelligent and powerful thought her worthy of respect. Even her thoughts were silenced by the surety in his gaze. In his words. They felt like the truth, not just opinion, and Rella believed them.

His regard didn't frighten her; it made her eager, though for what, she wasn't sure. Only that this feeling of enough was tied to Satrasi—the way he made her feel, the way he found value in her, the way he let her be.

When he broke eye contact to reach for another handful of salt, Rella felt the sting of disappointment even as the rest of her surroundings made themselves known once more. The rock digging into her knees, the breeze cooling the sweat on the back of her neck, the exhaustion in her bones from traveling too far while carrying heavy things. Rella slumped, adjusting her position to a more comfortable one.

While she refilled her waterskin and sipped from it, Satrasi finished off the first bag of salt. He paused then, eyes flicking over to her, drawing along her frame in a way that made her want to fidget even though she didn't want him to stop.

"Thank you," Satrasi said, as intense as before.

She didn't know what to say, so she settled for a nod.

Amusement crept back into his eyes at her discomfort. "I'll need to rest now, and absorb the rest of this." He motioned to the bags of salt. "After that, even if no one has come for me, I should have strength enough to go myself and return with your reward."

"Right." Rella nodded: he'd said as much before she left on her quest. "If you go on your own, perhaps it might be easiest if I went with you." Rella shrugged, only half sincere when she added, "Quickest way to ensure payment."

He smirked, likely seeing through to her true motivation—that she simply wanted to go with him. "Of course."

Rella's eyes widened when a thick black tentacle flowed out of the water behind him to wrap around the remaining bags of salt, drawing them behind him. She supposed that answered her unasked question about how strangely Satrasi's shadow and shape moved in the water.

"Until then," the sea demon said as he sank under the water and out of sight.

The next day, when Rella came back to the cave from foraging, it felt emptier than before. She found the crudely drawn map she'd left with Wicklow under the rock where she'd sat to talk with Satrasi. She hoped that meant Wicklow had managed to find his way here and not someone else: there was certainly no sign of a struggle.

Rella felt bereft, even if this was potentially an ideal outcome.

Since Rella had asked Dietha to meet her at the inn, she left the cave and returned to town. The innkeeper and her children often had extra work, and they paid well enough. That way, Rella could earn some coin, and maybe, if she was lucky, run into people from out of town.

There wasn't much for Rella to do this time around, but right as the innkeeper was about to send her on her way, a group with plenty of coin arrived. They were demanding and intimidating enough that they could only be mercenaries, and the innkeeper had Rella serve them instead of her own children.

Rella understood her caution even as she resented being the sacrificial lamb. Thankfully, she quickly figured out the mercenaries were here for a bounty, one for a demon pirate who could only be Satrasi. Now Rella had to keep her head down and try to draw as little attention as possible so she could learn what they knew—and what they had at their disposal—so she could warn him.

It was easy enough to skirt their notice at first since she'd made herself look younger as she always did. They paid her little heed as she refilled mugs and brought them food while they discussed their plans.

"I'll set the spell up tonight, and in the morning we'll know of any demons in a two-league radius. Tiny shithole like this with folk jumpy just at the sight of us"—the leader in a brown jacket jerked his head at the barkeep, who froze at the attention, causing him to smirk—"no chance there are any demons around beside the ones we're looking for. 'Sides, demons always got people who'll pay well for 'em. We'll move onto the next hole in the ground if he ain't here."

"That's all well and good, but that's not 'til morning," a woman in a blue dress whined. She was the youngest in the group, though the knives that decorated her entire body made it clear she wasn't to be underestimated. "What are we supposed to do until then? We're the most exciting thing here."

One of the other men batted his eyelashes at her while Rella collected mugs and plates as quietly as she could. "You could always do one of us."

Blue Dress made a face and threw a roll at him, which he caught and took a big bite out of with a grin. She scowled down at her stew. "Proving my point. Nothing else here worth anything."

"It does seem to just be mice here, scurrying to stay out of our sight while still taking our coin," an older blonde woman said, scowling as well.

Rella hated the way she eyed her ax and shared a mean smirk with the second man. People this strong, used to roaming and fighting and taking what they wanted, were nothing but trouble.

"No respect, just fear. Makes me wanna give 'em something to really be afraid of." Blue Dress fingered one of her many knives.

"Y'all are too used to the city. Plenty of fun to be had in the countryside; you just gotta be better at finding it. Gotta sneak up on these wary folk. Ain't that right, girl?" The leader's hand flashed out quick as lightning to snag Rella's apron.

She froze, cursing herself for not moving quicker, for not getting out once she heard about the spell.

"Really?" Blue Dress said, eyeing Rella up and down, unimpressed. "Her? She's still a child."

"No, I don't think so," the blonde replied.

Rella felt as if the older woman could see right through her, and she hated how bare it made her feel.

Her gaze was cold and dismissive as she continued, "She's at least of age. Nothing to her though—like as not to snap if you try to play with her."

"You're all too harsh," the man in charge—the one keeping Rella there—said, still too cheerful by half. "What do you say, lass? I'm sure you're itchin' to show someone you're all grown up." His eyes dragged down her body, lingering on her chest.

She despised him for it even though she tried not to show it. Telling him 'no' wouldn't get this sort to let her go. He might sound willing to compromise, but he wasn't; he wouldn't have grabbed her if he were.

He leered at her. "I promise no one from this backwater will give you as good a ride as I can."

Some of the others laughed while Rella looked down, not making eye contact with any of them. Her mind raced as his fingers tightened in her apron, fisting in the material to keep her close by. It was past time to get out of here, and her eyes darted to the exits, to check who might be in the way. Her fingers twitched to untie her apron strings and flee, but she knew these were hunters and she'd only get one chance.

She needed a—

The heavy door to the inn burst open, hitting the wall with a solid thunk. Everyone turned to look; a few, herself included, flinched at the sound, but her fingers were quick since she'd not get a better distraction. Two flicks, and all the mercenary was holding was the apron. Rella scurried to the other side of the fireplace, where the fireplace irons were within easy reach.

A shadow crossed in front of the door, and a woman, backlit by the sun so Rella couldn't make out her features, stuck her head in. "You sure this is the place, Captain? Seems rather"—her eyes landed on the cowering innkeeper and she grinned, displaying sharp teeth which betrayed her demon ancestor—"quaint." There was a threat to her words—as though by her presence she planned to change that quaintness.

"Yer the one who wanted to nab beds afore we got down to business." A man followed her in, exasperated.

Rella's eyes widened. They were both pirates: the smell of brine, the fit of their coats, the weathered skin and wind-tousled hair all told that. But one seemed familiar somehow. Her mouth almost dropped open as she identified *Wicklow*. With no slur to his voice, his eyes sharp and his frame tensed for a fight, wearing a smart black waistcoat and blue overcoat... Why, he nearly looked respectable! For the first time, Rella thought she saw what Satrasi must in him.

As if summoned by her thinking his name, another, bigger shadow appeared and followed them in. "We're already here," a new voice grumbled, deep and rolling, like the bells of the church that rang loud enough Rella felt them in her bones. Without the wet, echo-y quality his voice had had in the cave, Satrasi's voice was clear. "Just make it quick."

When Satrasi strode into view, the first thing Rella latched onto were his eyes. She hadn't realized how much she'd gotten used to them being half-closed and dim until she saw them now. His main eyes were a little bigger than her own, while his second set—less than half the size of the first right next to them—were also wide open. All four eyes glowed in the shadows falling on his face, vibrant red with pure black pupils, Now fully open, they gleamed with a preternatural light like rubies set with onyx.

They led her gaze to the red scales, like large freckles except they glowed too, scattered in clusters near those eyes and across all the other bare skin she could see. Speaking of, gone was the sickly pallor his skin once had. Whereas before his skin had been dull gray, now it was a dark, rich blue, which lightened on his underarms and the top of his chest.

He was more solid, more steady: healthy. He had been so amorphous in the water. Now the bright blue tentacles of his hair moved more than a breeze should allow them to, just as they had in water. Only the tentacles on his back that she knew must be there, though she couldn't see them, remained dark as ink. They melded with the shadows, leaving them as mysterious as before.

The brilliant red overcoat, which complemented his magnificent coloring, had no sleeves, revealing a crisp white shirt underneath. The shirt sleeves only went down to his elbows so that the fins on his forearms were left visible. They were so much more vibrant compared to how limp and colorless they had been in her memory. Their red and blue streaks brought to her mind jewelry or tattoos. Adornments.

Rella's eyes traveled down to his black breeches. The garment startled her. Yes, he'd said he had legs. And yet, it was still surprising to see them, defined and enclosed in tall black leather boots.

In addition to the physical improvements, Satrasi's presence had changed. Gone was the skulking predator, hovering just out of her reach, even when Rella knew she was within his. Now he stood before her, instantly in command of the room, the biggest threat.

He searched the room, looking for anything that might disagree with that assessment, welcoming the challenge such a creature might offer him. He rolled back his shoulders, almost restlessly, as if he couldn't understand why he might be in such a small space so unable to contain him. How obvious it was that those fools who had captured him in the first place never would have been able to keep him caged for long.

He pinpointed the closest thing this place had to a threat; the mercenaries. A hungry grin spread across his face, his teeth glinting silver. "Well now, looks as though we aren't the only guests gracing this humble town."

The mercenaries had frozen where they sat except to put hands on hilts. The leader's eyes darted to the silver in Satrasi's outfit—the silver braid that went from his shoulder to his chest, a reference to his title of "the Admiral"—and then to his belt buckle, which had the skull and tentacles that was his insignia.

He clearly knew exactly who this was. "Always interesting to meet others passing through the backcountry. What brings you to these parts?" The leader had to be trying to pretend Satrasi wasn't why his group was here.

Nothing in the mercenary's demeanor gave him away, but Satrasi was no fool. He shrugged. "You know how it is, handling my end of a deal. You?"

"On our way to meet some lord in the port. High-paying bounty. You know how it is," the mercenary parroted with a sneer.

"Of course. No one that I might know though, was it?"

"We only hunt on land, though I'm surprised to see your ilk so far from the sea."

"Deals are deals," Satrasi replied, "wherever they take us."

"I'll drink to that," one of the other mercenaries said.

"Care to join us?" the woman in blue offered with a wicked glint in her eye that might have been flirty but mostly came across as predatory. "I'm sure you'll prove more interesting than the mudlappers here."

The woman who'd come with Satrasi grinned and spread her hands. "Surely they're not so bad. Small town folks are always so sweet to passers-through."

"Unless they got cause not to be," Wicklow said, his eyes flicking to the still-frozen figure of the innkeeper, who seemed fearful of yet more dangerous strangers, and the boy, who leapt behind the kitchen door as soon as there was notice on him.

"We've been nothing but polite," the mercenary leader lied.

"That true, little bite?"

Rella's eyes flicked to Satrasi's face in surprise and found his locked on her. He smirked, and she felt the last bits of lingering anxiety settle. Of course he saw these folks for what they were, and he was here to hold up his end of the deal with her. Rella's building trust in him solidified into something strong and powerful.

Satrasi's eyes turned to the lead mercenary, not bothering to watch Rella scurry over to him—she drew one of the fireplace pokers from their stand, skirting the mercenaries' table to be by Satrasi's side.

"Because I'd bet a pretty penny on that being her apron in your hand." He nodded at the material the mercenary had forgotten he still held, judging by the double take he gave the white cotton cloth.

"It is," Rella said, speaking to Satrasi alone, because no one else here mattered. His eyes dropped down to her as she fit herself comfortably next to him. She was so used to him being below her in the water, and now he stood nearly a head taller than her. It made her feel safer. "They were starting to push, but no, they hadn't done nothing yet. You should know they're here looking for you."

His eyebrows rose in interest, his voice even more darkly amused. "Oh, are they?"

The thud of a mug hitting the table made her twitch, but Satrasi didn't give any sign he heard, his eyes still on Rella.

"This fluffhead girl doesn't know what she's talking about," the lead mercenary growled as he leaned back in his chair. "Why would we be looking for you?" he asked, trying for casual, but that facade as cracking. "You just got here, and we've been here for more than a day."

"Why *are* they looking for me?" Satrasi asked Rella, his expression inviting her to be in on the joke.

It was warming, to be listened to, to be part of a group. To know Satrasi would believe her above others. She felt nearly drunk on the confidence it gave her. "A page escaped you and the forest demon. Governor offered them a hundred gold for you alive, half if dead."

"That's up from last year," Wicklow said, amused. "Getting frustrated, it seems."

"They have a spell map—finds demons in a two-league radius, they said. Were about to set it and find you in the morn." She ignored the curses from the mercenaries, who gave up on their paper-thin ruse now that it was clear how much she'd overheard.

"Well now, isn't that interesting?" Satrasi's eyes flew to the mercenaries, who were getting to their feet with weapons drawn. "Seems I owe you even more than I thought. Why don't you fetch the rest of my people from outside so we can take care of this little annoyance and relieve them of their oh-so-intriguing map?"

That was too much for the mercenaries, who lunged for the pirates. Rella nodded to Satrasi and dashed outside, where she found Hayleth—the half-demon from the tavern in the port—leaning by some horses with three other pirates. "Fight broke out with some mercenaries looking for your captain," Rella told them.

Even Hayleth, who hadn't liked or trusted her previously, moved as soon as the first few words left her mouth, or maybe he could hear the sound of furniture being knocked about.

Rella vibrated with energy, wanting to help with the fight but knowing she'd only get in the way. She got down on one knee by the still-open door to the inn, iron poker in hand. Sure enough, as the fighting started to die down, someone rushed out. After the split second it took her to identify the head mercenary, she brought the poker up with both hands to strike him below his knees. He roared. The force nearly threw her to the ground, but she was able to right herself and scramble back as he went sprawling.

Before Rella could worry about getting away from him before he got up, a long black tentacle whipped past her, wrapped around the mercenary's belt, and dragged his prone form into the inn. Satrasi was in the doorway, a full-blown grin on his face displaying those sharp, sharp teeth. He pulled the leader behind him, tossing, "Find out where he's got the map," over his shoulder. He barely looked like he'd been in a fight, clothing in fine order, no blood or injuries on him, only his unsheathed sword a concession toward any danger.

Satrasi's eyes landed on Rella. "You simply can't help being impressive, can you? I've got your payment." He patted his breast pocket. "But more than that: how'd you like to join my crew? I could use a messenger like you." He held out a hand to help her to her feet.

Rella didn't even need to think as she clasped Satrasi's hand. "Yes."

CHAPTER SIX

Present Day

Rella wakes with an aching throat but also with the sense of calm and belonging that only comes from being in her rooms. Even when she said 'yes' to becoming Satrasi's messenger, she never could have imagined how content and exciting—how satisfying and safe—her life would be. From her first few lessons on sailing, to the seizure of the carrier, and finally to missions farther and wider than she'd previously been aware existed. And through it all, Satrasi's commanding presence: always trusting her, always behind her, never underestimating her. The dream was an unnecessary—but comforting—reminder of the truth she knows best in this world: she can count on Satrasi.

Rella goes about her morning as usual, except she takes another dose of medicine and wraps some more cold cloths around her neck. Then she catches up on some minor mending until it's time for today's meeting.

When she saw Satrasi yesterday to get her orders regarding Critchley, he more or less said Wicklow was still managing the day-to-day of the fleet. Rella hopes that means Satrasi might have more personal work for her soon. As happy as she is to help with general fleet communications, she's always enjoyed being one of the only people Satrasi trusts with his private messages.

Anticipation thrums through her as she gets ready. She's glad no drink or other mess ended up on her overcoat, and the only real concession to her injury she needs is loosening the lace of her shirt by her neck as well as adjusting her coat collar so there's no fabric against her throat. A glance in the mirror shows her throat is still covered in mottled bruises ranging from red to pink with hints of purple starting to creep in, so there's no hiding what happened.

Not that she planned on doing so.

She slips into the large hall below deck without fanfare. Leaning against the shaded wall near the back corner, she settles in to wait. Sometimes she chats or hangs around with the other messengers or crew she's friendly with, but today she keeps to herself, not wanting to discuss what happened with anyone—or to talk at all, really.

Everyone must be able to read her mood or has heard the gossip, as their eyes slide past her even easier than usual. Of course, it could be that nearly half of them are hungover. She's never understood why. This meeting wasn't a surprise; isn't it rough enough being awake this early without a pounding in one's head? At least the throbbing of her throat isn't her fault.

When Admiral Satrasi strides in to sit behind his desk, she isn't even looking up. She simply senses his presence. His magnetism resonates in her bones whenever he's near. She spoke with him only yesterday, but they've still been too long apart, and so her eyes are drawn to him like one dying of thirst in a desert to an oasis. His trip has invigorated him, magnified him, and it makes something in her blood eager and hungry.

Reluctantly, she pulls her eyes from him to the other captains present. They're arranged in a semicircle in front of his desk, ready to give their reports, and she focuses on them in a vain attempt to regain her self-control.

The local captains are here in person, and after their reports, the messengers for those further out at sea will supply their communications until the status and position of the entire fleet is updated. As all Rella did was talk to a local, potential recruit, she'll submit her report near the end. After all, her message is not supposed to be anything more than giving an exact time for when the admiral will be meeting with Captain Critchley in a few days' time.

She makes a game out of guessing who Satrasi will send where as they all report, but as the minutes pass, Rella picks up on murmurs and glances her way. Either some have noticed her throat or they've heard what happened; with people coming and going as business carries on, she's not surprised that word is spreading. She pays the whispers no mind, too busy luxuriating in Satrasi's presence to care. Besides, it's not like rumors won't fly once Critchley is dealt with.

Rella moves further along the wall as her time to report comes nigh. Usually, she is unobtrusive and overlooked, crowded without others realizing they're even doing so. Today she's given plenty of space.

"New ships?" one of the captains says in response to a comment from Satrasi. "The *Lash's Revenge* is still a clip away, but the *Lux Lady* arrived yesterday."

"Yes, I know," the admiral says, eyes on the note he's writing.

Rella pushes off the wall on cue and slips between the captains and other messengers to stand in front of his desk. She clasps her hands behind her back because they're shaking for some reason.

"Messenger, report," he says.

"Captain Critchley of the *Lux Lady*," Rella says, her voice far rougher and raspier than even yesterday—all those nearby turn, if they hadn't already been watching. But her gaze is fixed on Satrasi, who goes still after the first syllable leaves her lips. She swallows; it doesn't help. "Has proven rather uncooperative."

He raises his head slowly, and his red, red eyes fix on her neck. He lowers his pen gently to the desktop. Only the navy tentacles on his head betray any agitation. Although the sudden weight and pressure in the air might also be his doing. "You'd no mark on you yesterday." His voice is deadly, soft and low. "Who did this to you?"

"When I spoke with Captain Critchley in the Saucy Siren," Rella says, resisting the urge to place a hand on her neck because it aches something fierce with her talking—her voice is like sandpaper, for all she fights to keep it as intelligible as possible—"he was displeased that you couldn't see him for another two days."

"He did this to you? *Here*?"

She's not heard Satrasi this angry in years. Unlike common hotheads, when Satrasi is angry, he gets calm and deliberate. Inevitable. Perhaps Rella shouldn't take so much joy and satisfaction that he's already become the eye of the storm, but she left usual morals behind when she signed on with pirates—if not earlier. She has no pretenses with herself. She welcomes the heat of his regard and the frigidity of his fury equally.

"Yes," Rella replies, unable to stop her eyes from roaming his features, seeing how they harden, how his demeanor sharpens further. The muscle in his jaw ticks and there's a layer of incredulity to his anger, same as she felt last night. "I had to draw my blade for him to release me."

Satrasi leans back in his chair, eyes still on her throat: he's not looked away from the bruises since he first lifted his head at the sound of her voice. "Tell me."

"I informed him of the times you were available, but he wanted to meet sooner. He thought he deserved to be seen more quickly. He pushed for today."

It's fascinating to watch the subtle twitches under his skin as he holds himself still. It's clear he's weighing what the appropriate recompense for the arrogant captain will be. Despite the rasp, Rella's voice is even, giving away little of her thoughts. Satrasi doesn't need to hear them to know how she thinks. He's always seen her so clearly.

"I explained that today wasn't an option. He insisted and then grabbed me by the throat. The rest of the billiard room drew on him, but my blade is what prompted him to release me."

He's somewhat mollified by the news that others moved to protect her even as his lip curls in disgust at Critchley's behavior. The frills on his forearms are rigid, his hair tentacles restless, and his eyes glow far brighter than usual.

"He refused to give any answer aside from today," she continues. "Said he was too important to be kept waiting."

That finally prompts Satrasi's eyes to meet her own. His eyes are vibrant red and deep black, almost seeming to swirl with the intensity of outrage in them. "Did he now?"

Satrasi crooks a finger, and Rella steps closer without needing to think, mesmerized as always by him. He leans forward to meet her; once close enough, he reaches for her. His touch is so light she feels coolness, more than pressure, when he rests his fingers against the marks on her neck.

Goosebumps race across her skin at the barely-there touch, and lightning zips through her veins as his thumb strokes whisper light against the base of her throat. She takes no care to breathe shallowly, craving his skin against hers.

Slowly he withdraws his hand, and she swallows to keep from letting out a bereft noise. It curls at the back of her throat, unspoken, as his eyes meet hers once more. There's a question in his gaze, but whatever is in hers answers him. He nods very slowly and leans back in his chair. She mirrors the motion, straightening as she waits for his decision.

Without looking away from her, he jerks a hand to another person standing off to his right. "Very well. He wants to meet me today?" His voice is low and resonant; everyone in the room can hear him easily because it's gone silent enough that a dropped pin would sound like a cannonball. "I suppose, just this once, we can grant his wish."

Rella smiles in response to the slow smirk spreading across his face.

"Take five crew and bring Captain Critchley of the *Lux Lady* to me. Now. No coercion will be needed, I'm sure, nor should it be used unless necessary." Satrasi's voice is as self-assured as she's ever heard it. "He'll come of his own volition. After all, he asked for this."

The silence disappears as they wait for Critchley. Rella accepts the water someone hands her but refuses all medical aid. She wants Critchley to have to face the full damage. Regardless of whether or not he'll care, it makes her feel more justified. At the very least, everyone else *does* care: people keep sneaking glances at her neck, and there's a background hum of angry murmurs.

When Critchley arrives, it's clear he has no notion he's in trouble. The smug curl to his lips shows his belief that he truly is important enough to warrant a next-day meeting. That he can make demands of Satrasi. His gaze sweeps the room; he's pleased with the audience, preening at the sight of the fleet captains. He's not even affected by any sort of hangover. He must have slept like a babe.

The only thing that gives him pause, for even a second, is the sight of Satrasi in all his inhuman glory. Rella observed that there were no sea demons among his crew, which isn't impossible—demons aren't that common on ships new to piracy—but they're less rare among those living on the edges of society than within it. All of his crew were men too—which is even less common.

An older man with a well-kept but full beard has been escorted here along with Critchley. He has the weathered look of someone who's worked on ships his whole life. She doesn't recognize him, so he must have been watching the *Lux Lady* last night, not at the Saucy Siren.

He's far more wary than Critchley, keeping a close eye on the ones who brought them here. He seems to at least suspect they're guards, not helpful escorts. He's also better able to read a room; his shoulders tense as soon as he's through the doors. His hand strays toward his gun before he stops himself, realizing that might be seen as a threat. His instincts are screaming at him, and he's listening.

Critchley dismisses the rest of the assembled audience, striding to stand in front of Satrasi's desk. While he does so, Takis, the first mate of the *Hungry Serpent,* slips into the hall. Their eyes find hers immediately and they wink.

Once his first mate catches up to stand at his shoulder, Critchley inclines his head in greeting. "Captain Critchley of the *Lux Lady*. A pleasure to meet you, Admiral Satrasi."

"Yes, Captain Critchley. Your reputation precedes you." Satrasi leans back in his chair, appearing nonchalant.

But Rella's eyes trace the tension in his muscles that betray his iron control.

"Our latest victory over the SS *Wisdom* was rather impressive, if I do say so myself," Critchley replies.

Critchley obviously thinks Satrasi is referring to whatever naval battle and subsequent booty landed him his interview for the fleet in the first place. It's fairly entertaining watching him make all the wrong assumptions.

"Captain Jack certainly took notice, but that was not what I was referring to," Satrasi corrects mildly.

Critchley frowns, some of his arrogance diminished. "While I admit we've had some other decent scores, none were as successful." He gives a careless wave of his hand. "You know how it is when you start out, lots of small fish. What else have you heard? I'm afraid it might be mere rumor."

"That's precisely what I'd like to determine. You see, it seems as though there might have been some sort of"—Satrasi pauses as if thinking—"*misunderstanding* with my messenger last night."

Critchley's eyebrows rise and a flash of contempt flickers over his face.

Rella knows her cue, she steps forward.

Critchley's eyes land on her, and there's a brief hesitation in his expression as he realizes he has to make a decision. He's no longer in a tavern plied with alcohol; he's gotten what he thinks he wants: a meeting with Satrasi today. He can back off without doubling down on his treatment of her. He can say he was drunk, that he did misunderstand, that he wasn't aware she was a personal messenger and not someone having him on. However, he sneers at her instead, his eyes lingering on the bruises on her throat. Not with regret, but with satisfaction.

"I don't know what that one told you, but I'm sure it was a lie," he says, jerking his thumb at Rella as he turns to face Satrasi. "She was refusing to do her job and didn't know her place. Not sure if she was trying to delay my joining your fleet or if someone paid her to do so against you, but she was putting off our meeting. Trying to make me wait days when, of course, you'd want to see me far sooner. And when someone ain't listening to me"—Critchley gives a careless shrug and smirks at her—"I *make* them listen." He turns back to Satrasi. "The lying chit has more guts than I thought, to try to turn it around on me by tattling and whining in your ear."

Satrasi nods slowly. Rella wonders if he's ever met someone who so hugely underestimated the situation he found himself in, who kept digging himself in deeper while remaining blissfully unaware of what he was doing. She certainly hasn't.

Given his expression of surprise and worry, this is the first time the first mate has heard this story. Between his knowledge of his captain and his ability to read between the lines, he must suspect what truly went down. His hand finds a religious pendant of some kind that hangs around his neck, but he stays silent, waiting in trepidation.

Good, Rella thinks, *at least one of them is worried*.

"I see," Satrasi says after a second's pause, as if wanting to be sure Critchley's done spewing bile. "Well, I've heard her side and now I've heard yours. I'm sure I don't have to tell you they don't agree."

Critchley grins, mistaking which side of the joke he's on.

"Admiral, if I might speak?" Takis steps forward. They seem worried about stepping in without the admiral's say-so but determined to speak if permitted. Did they care this much about her? Or was it the justice of the matter? Or some blend of the two? Rella makes a note to do them a good turn in reply. "I was there last night. Heard the whole thing."

"Takis of the *Hungry Serpent*," Satrasi acknowledges and waves them closer. "Yes, if you'd like."

"Thank ye kindly," they say with a rough bow to Satrasi. "I've not heard what the Marlin told you today and I've no notion of what your orders were, and I'll not guess at that, but there was no lip or rudeness on the Marlin's side of things. Said you couldn't see 'im until three days' time. Two days' now, I suppose, and he"—they jerk their chin toward Critchley—"said he wanted to meet today. They were at a standstill, both gettin' frustrated with the other. Marlin Rella made no motion to attack, and the captain gave no warning. Only let go of 'er throat when 'er blade was put to his skin."

"You sleepin' with this whore?" Critchley cuts in, going for condescending, but for the first time it's a veneer to cover up some trepidation. He can't stop his eyes from darting to Satrasi's face to see his reaction. The lack of one only makes him more nervous.

Takis sneers at him. "Wouldn't matter if I were. I'm only tellin' how things went."

"Thank you, Takis," Satrasi says, bringing both of their focuses to him. "I appreciate your stopping by to lend your voice to this matter."

Critchley clearly wants to object to such a kind description to what he basically called slander. But he doesn't even get the chance to open his mouth.

"Captain Critchley." Satrasi leans forward, elbows on the desk, fingers laced together. "'Admiral' is not just a title I took to spark fear in the easily persuaded. My fleet is what makes me the Admiral—the myriad captains and crew who answer to me are where my power comes from. I command the best, the fastest, the strongest, and the smartest this side of the Unbroken Sea. The only other who compares is the Commander of the Red Flag Fleet in the east, and I plan to sail as far from her as I can. We're no mere coalition, loosely held together by mutual self-interest." Satrasi's gaze is unwavering, his voice commanding. "We are still here because we are one unit, one enemy that no nation can match. This is my fleet, and I am its *admiral*."

"I know this." Critchley sounds both annoyed and pleading, his arrogant attitude at war with the prickling awareness that he's in danger. He must be realizing that this conversation is not going to go his way. "That's why I seek to join in the first place. You don't need to convince me of your greatness."

"And yet you do not seem to have the faintest comprehension of that which you claim to wish to join." Satrasi is no longer pretending to not be angry. "Do you know how many ships I have under my command already? Do you know how many petitions to join up I get? Do you know how many I could take, if I so desired? Ships are not what I lack. Bodies are not what I lack. And because I have numbers, I can afford to be particular in who I allow to join up. Intelligence, loyalty, novelty—people who have summat new and therefore valuable to bring to me, that is who I seek."

Satrasi continues, his voice so powerful that Critchley couldn't interrupt if he wanted to, "The actual challenge of managing my fleet? It's *communication*. Ensuring my captains know what their orders are, ensuring they have the most current information, that they know of changing tides and needs. Not only do I need speed in communication, but I need trust. I need to know that I have those who are loyal and competent to bring my messages where they need to go. I don't let anyone take on that role without years of service, until they have proven themselves worthy. My elite messengers are my organization's lifeblood."

Pride sings through her veins at such a generous and explicit description of how much Satrasi values her and the other messengers—and at how Critchley has lost all color in his face.

"They are my sincerest representatives. When they speak, it is with *my* words; when they answer, it is with *my* words." Satrasi punctuates each "my" with the jab of a finger at the desk, and Critchley flinches both times.

"Whatever is done to them in the course of their duties is done to *me*. And you brutalized one of them, on my protected grounds, out of pettiness and an overly inflated sense of your own importance." Satrasi's hair tentacles whip around as if in a stiff sea breeze.

Critchley's face contorts into a fearful mask. His knees have certainly locked in place, likely the only reason he's still standing. His eyes are wide, pupils dilated.

Rella has never known if Satrasi has additional intimidation at his disposal due to his nature, but she's sure he doesn't need it.

"You've got no distinction, you've no interesting booty, you've no particular coin to your name." Satrasi has escalated to hitting his desk with a flat palm with each point, and Critchley jumps each time. "And now I've seen you've no brains in your empty head, only hot air. I've no need of such a person in my fleet." Satrasi smiles, but it's only to better display his sharp teeth. There's no remorse or indecision in his face. "So, I'm afraid I'll have to decline your petition to join, and I'll be taking the *Lux Lady* and her crew as recompense for the grievous insult done to myself and my messenger."

Critchley starts to protest. Rella can't make out any individual words, only his desperation and fear and outrage all bubbling up and over each other.

Satrasi merely shakes his head, almost gently, as he says, "No, no, your presence is no longer required."

Quick and silent as shadows, two black tentacles move out from behind Satrasi and snap his neck. Critchley's body falls to the ground like a marionette with its strings cut, and Satrasi's tentacles retreat behind him, out of sight, but at the forefront of everyone's minds.

"Wicklow," Satrasi says, eyes back on his paperwork. "Strip the *Lux Lady* and her crew of anything of value, then dump the crew at the nearest port." He smirks at Rella. "You can have first pick."

She smiles and nods her thanks, wincing slightly at the way the motion causes her neck to ache.

His eyes spark as he frowns, eyes flicking down to stare at the paperwork on his desk once more. "Who's on our shortlist of new captains?"

Wicklow slides a list over to Satrasi.

If Critchley's first mate could have gotten any paler, he would have. "Admiral, sir, I beg your mercy. I understand that C-Critchley's disrespect required action, but the rest of the crew did nothing."

"Correct. They did nothing while my messenger was assaulted," Satrasi replies. "Be grateful you do not share his fate."

"Admiral—" The first mate falls silent at a glare from Satrasi before he licks his lips, words hovering on his tongue. But all he says in the end is, "He was our captain, sir."

Satrasi's eyes are sharp as he looks the man over. "Very well, inform the first mate of the *Huzzah* that she is now the captain of the *Lux Lady*. She can have her pick of the crew, and the rest can be given scut work on the carrier until we figure out what else to do with them. Any who wish to go ashore can. Any who object, throw them into the sea." Satrasi points at the first mate. "It's up to you to impress upon your crewmates what their options are, understood?"

"Yes, sir." The first mate gives a jerky bow, aware of the precarious position he's in. "Thank you, sir."

"Take him back to his ship and inform the crew," Satrasi orders those who brought the *Lux Lady* men here. "Then tell Jimena of her new command."

They agree easily, and the first mate leaves with them without any fuss. After they leave, Satrasi's eyes flick to the body and then to one of the crew nearby. "Tollen, clean that up. You can have whatever you want off him."

Tollen bows, eyes already on Critchley's silver, and Rella figures his body will be fed to one of Satrasi's demon pets that swim near whatever vessel he's on.

Satrasi hands Wicklow some sheaves of paper, noting the change in positions and the new ship to the fleet while the rest of the room waits quietly. When Wicklow straightens with a nod and the papers in hand, Satrasi pushes away from his desk. "This has already been a more disruptive day than I wished for," Satrasi says with a scowl. He flaps his hand at the room at large. "Back to your duties." He points at Rella before she moves. "Except for you, my messenger. Stay."

"Of course."

The others leave without fanfare, with only Wicklow stopping to ask: "You want me to send a doctor to ye?" His face is serious, but his eyes are kind when they dart to hers.

Satrasi shakes his head. "Not necessary." He stands and beckons Rella to follow him into his private office. "Come with me."

CHAPTER SEVEN

Rella follows Satrasi into his private office. It's rare for them to be alone.

It's also rare that he shuts the door behind her. It makes being here more private, more intimate. Instead of going behind the desk, he ushers Rella over to a corner of the room near the liquor cabinet.

Whenever she's in close quarters with Satrasi, his height is suddenly all she can think of: it feels like he could wrap around her completely. His scent envelops her, a cooling, sea breeze sort of smell—all the sharp tang of the ocean without the heavy, cloying, occasionally rank scent that accompanied things that have been immersed in seawater for too long.

Satrasi comes to a stop, and she mirrors the motion, attuned to him as always.

"Let's take a closer look," he says, carefully reaching for her.

She bares her throat to him without thought, wondering if he'll notice the way her pulse jumps and her breathing shallows.

Over the last few months, she's been away on longer missions, gathering news from the more distantly flung ships then reporting back only to head out again almost immediately. She's missed him. She hopes they'll be back to spending more time together now that he's home. Especially since she's certain his most recent journey has been a success and whatever demon magic he's sought has been found. There's an additional thrum to his presence, something new. It only makes her want to soak up his aura more.

She understands his need to recover, that he's been spending long hours soaking in the sea, but she hopes he plans to stay on the carrier for a time. She hopes he keeps her here too. She wants to be a cat, lying in the sun, but instead of sunlight she requires only Satrasi's presence.

Rella snaps out of her thoughts when his fingers press gently along her throat, pushing the collar of her overcoat to the side. Gripping her chin with his other hand, he tilts it so he can more closely examine the marks that mar her flesh and lets out a hiss. She sighs, his fingers cooler and soothing atop the ache.

When he pulls back, her eyelids flutter open. Rella's not even sure when she closed them.

"You're too short, little messenger," he says with a faint smirk. "Let's fix that, hm?"

He gestures to her right, but she's already nodding without bothering to think about it. She trusts him, and it's so nice to have someone else tending her wounds. He's the only one she truly trusts to do so. She'll agree to anything if he asks, especially if he keeps his firm hands on her.

He chooses that moment to let go of her. Rella blinks, abruptly bereft, his absence is a cold breeze that wakes her up. She opens her mouth to ask why when his hands land on her hips. A squeak of surprise escapes when he lifts her up and sets her down on top of the table.

Satrasi chuckles. His face is far closer than before; the table he put her on leaves her only a couple inches lower than him. "Much better," he says, so close his low voice vibrates through where her hands are clinging to his forearms instead of through the air. When he lets go of her hips, she reluctantly lets go of him as well.

His hands at least return to her, one to tilt her head back and the other to hold her overcoat aside. "Be easier if I move this out of the way."

"Sure," Rella says and then winces at how her voice sounds—grating and rough—as well as how raw her throat is.

A flash of anger seems to pass through Satrasi at the reminder of how damaged her voice is. Through where they're touching, she can feel a sort of thrum, a blend between a low growl and a purr. It's immensely soothing, sending a strange sort of calm down her spine, warming her with his regard.

One of his large hands pushes at her overcoat until she gets the hint and helps him help her out of it. She supposes it's easier than holding the collar back, but she can't stop the goosebumps that spread across her skin at Satrasi undressing her in any capacity. She's seen him partially-undressed, most often when returning with messages that needed to be relayed to him immediately. But the reverse hasn't happened. Not that taking her coat off is particularly revealing—she's still got her waistcoat and shirt on—but him removing any piece of her clothing is enough to send her thoughts tumbling.

Of course, once that's done, Satrasi pulls back entirely. Draping her coat over the back of his chair, he opens the locked cabinet next to the liquor cabinet and pulls something out. "Here." He hands her a flask. The metal is cool—maybe it came from an icebox? She unscrews the top as he explains, "This should help soothe and heal your throat."

Bringing the flask to her lips, she drinks. It's as cool as she expected but thicker than she's prepared for and almost... minty. After a few seconds, his hand closes over hers to tilt the flask away from her mouth. For a second it's almost too much, like her throat is closing, clogging up. She swallows determinedly as he pulls the vessel away to thrust another into her hand. She hurriedly downs the blessedly clear fresh water.

His eyes are trained on her throat as it moves. It's intoxicating to have him so close, so focused on her. Her chest feels tight with anticipatory excitement that grows with each second as Satrasi continues to stay so close.

"Better?" Satrasi murmurs as she finishes the water.

"Much," Rella replies, brushing the back of her hand against her mouth to catch a few small droplets.

Satrasi's eyes fly up to hers at the sound of her breathy but far clearer voice.

As she darts her tongue out to catch those drops off her finger, she swears the temperature in the room heats under his red gaze.

"Good," Satrasi says with satisfaction.

Rella suppresses a shiver, although she's not sure she manages to stop some heat from flooding her cheeks.

He smirks as if he can see right through her before his eyes return to her neck. "That should sort out most of the internal damage, but there's still the matter of this bruising." Satrasi's hand wraps around the back of her neck, away from the worst bruising, but lightly putting pressure on some of it with his fingers.

Her breath hitches and Satrasi lets go as soon as it does, his hands moving down to smooth along her shoulders. She appreciates the comforting gesture even as some part of her laments the loss of his firm grip. With the inside of her throat much, much better, her neck feels more like any other bruise she's received—only hurting when pressed.

"This never should have happened," he says, fury bleeding into his voice.

"Only did the one time," Rella says, because it's done and the one who did it has been dealt with. "It's not as though I was in any real danger."

"He could have snapped your neck before you or anyone else reacted," Satrasi says, his voice dark and dripping. His grip on her shoulders tightens ever so slightly, as if he's wishing he'd been there when Critchley laid hands on her in the first place.

"He didn't," Rella replies, because she can't think like that. She gave up on 'what ifs' when she found herself the lone survivor of a bandit attack, and she doesn't plan to go back. It's far simpler this way. "Anyone could kill anyone else most of the time, if they did so for no reason with no warning. That's life."

"Not here," Satrasi insists. "Not in my territory."

Rella smiles up at him. "No. That's why even someone as stupid and arrogant and hard-headed as him, with no notion of respect, didn't. Because some part of him knew he couldn't. Not here."

Satrasi stares at her, something indefinable in his eyes as he searches for something in her. She has no idea what that might be, but she lets him look his fill. Anything he'd like from her, anything she can give, is already his. He earns that from her every time he shows her respect. Every time he protects her, in person or by reputation. Every time he helps her make a home, make herself who she wants to be.

To say he loses tension in his frame would be wrong, but something shifts—in him—in the air. She knows he's letting the incident go and accepting her words as the truth they are.

Rella's smile softens. That loyalty he prizes works both ways: she knows who he is too. The others might think they do, but none can read him as she can. None can listen as well as she can. None can respond to his thoughts as well as she can.

He's *her* admiral, after all.

That something else in his gaze grows, distracting her, fascinating her. It's in the way his eyes rake up and down her form, checking her over. It's in the hold he still has on her shoulders. It's in the way his tongue—black with red streaks that seem to glow brighter than usual—wets his lips, flicks around his sharp teeth.

Whatever is building in him, she's content to wait him out. He's never let her down before, and she doubts he will now.

Until then...

Her eyes slip shut. Experimentally, she rolls her head around and feels a corresponding ache. Her hand automatically goes to touch her neck, but she ends up dropping it into her lap. She doesn't want anything in the way in case Satrasi wants to put his fingers back on her.

She opens her eyes lazily, having completed a sweep of her head and gotten a handle on how bad the ache is. She can live with it just fine and has had far worse.

Satrasi's eyes meet hers immediately, a question in them.

"Hurts, but not bad," Rella says without his needing to ask. "The inside was the worst part, my voice and throat."

He presses his lips together in disapproval. "You received this in the course of your duties for me," he says. The tentacles of his hair curling at the ends, but make no other movements. "I'll set it right, if you'll allow me?"

"Yes, of course." She focuses on not clenching her hands on her trousers out of eagerness for whatever Satrasi will do next. With his eyes on her throat, she tries to keep her breathing steady. A difficult proposition.

He leans in closer, lips practically brushing against her ear as he softly says, "Hold still." He cups both hands around her neck, his thumbs pushing up under her chin as his fingers wrap around her throat completely.

The hold makes her weak in the best possible way, wholly in his hands—quite literally. She hopes he attributes the stutter in her breathing to the slight pressure he uses, which certainly is the cause of a wince she can't help.

Her mouth falls open as she pulls in air, due to both the pressure and some minimal twinges of pain as well as a sort of wild excitement. As she tries to keep her eyes open, she catches an amused glint in all four of his as their glow increases, his black pupils growing deeper as specks of black appear in the red. She can't resist the urge to close her eyes and succumb to the weightlessness Satrasi's firm hold inspires. Rella's so aware of the bones of his fingers, his thumbs keeping her chin pointed up, how she can sense him bent over her, feel him like the heat from a fire. It's not heat though, it's something else: a presence, aura, power that rolls off of him in waves.

If anything, his hands grow cooler. Pronounced enough that a shiver dances down her spine, goosebumps rippling across her skin. That resonating hum from earlier has returned. The tips of his fingers curl ever so slightly at the back of her neck, sharp claws scraping delicately against the small hairs at the nape of her neck as a crescendo builds in the very air around them.

Rella feels the urge to sway, but Satrasi holds her fast. All she wants is for this moment to never end. She wants to be alone with Satrasi, his hands on her body, firm and safe in his grip. What could be better than this?

As if finally given permission, all the thoughts Rella usually keeps back flood her mind. All the ways he could touch her, all the ways he could send shivers down her spine and goosebumps across her skin, all the ways he could pull gasps from her lips. What noises could she draw from him if given the chance? What would he feel like under her fingertips? What new heights could they ascend to together?

Heat spills down her body to pool between her legs, and she can't help but raggedly inhale as she squirms, aching.

The hum cuts off all at once, and his hands warm up rapidly. Once they've returned to normal body temperature, he carefully pulls one hand away. "There we are." His voice has dropped even lower and does nothing to quell the heat she's drunk on.

His voice does prompt her to open her eyes, as does the light tracing of his fingers along her neck. No pain. She blinks, waking up slightly to the purpose of whatever he's done.

Satrasi moves his other thumb from its place under her chin to stroke along her jawline.

Her eyes seek his out, only to lose her entire train of thought when she meets them. His black pupils are larger than ever, his mouth open to display teeth and tongue. Distantly, she remembers being relieved when they first met that he didn't look hungry.

Rella's not certain she'd be able to say the same now.

Satrasi leans closer, one hand holding her still. Rella's practically breathing the same air when he says, voice rich with amusement, "Enjoy that, did you?"

Heat floods her cheeks.

"Is there something you'd like to tell me, little bite?"

He doesn't call her 'little bite' often these days, so she cherishes each time he does. This utterance of the endearment might be her new favorite, though.

His other hand pushes a strand of hair behind her ear. "Something you might *want*?"

She can't articulate a single thought in her head, possibly because there aren't any. Just feeling, just desire for... "*Satrasi.*"

She barely recognizes her own voice. It's practically a whine, breathy for an entirely new reason—one that has nothing to do with her throat.

It seems to be enough because he moves closer to her, forcing her knees further apart as his expression sharpens. He leans down to trace his nose along her throat and inhales.

Tension and anticipation flood her muscles as she tries not to shake with need.

His breath hits her ear. "I can smell it on you, like the finest perfume."

"*Satrasi*," she repeats, the truest plea she's ever made. She stays as still as she had when he first bade her to, worried a single wrong move might make this moment pop like a bubble, like a dream.

It's enough.

His grip on her tightens briefly as he lets out a little growl. Then he turns her face as he moves, and before she knows it, his lips are against hers in a languid, confident kiss.

For a second, she continues to hold still, too surprised this is actually happening. Then that tension bleeds out of her as she leans into him, finally letting her hands release their grip on her own clothing to tangle in his, keeping him close.

Those sharp teeth catch on her lower lip, and he immediately takes advantage of the way she obligingly opens her mouth.

He makes it so easy to get lost in the kiss. Heat suffuses through her entire body at the hot slide of his tongue against her own. The rising inferno is only further encouraged by his hand on her hip pulling her closer. This is more full body contact than she's ever had with Satrasi, and it isn't *enough*.

She makes a greedy, wanting noise in the back of her throat. Satrasi growls in response, sliding his hand from her jaw to cup the back of her head.

While she keeps one hand firmly wrapped around one of his lapels, the other moves down his solid chest, around his back, her fingernails scrabbling for purchase. She needs him closer, closer, *closer*.

She doesn't know how long his mouth moves against her own before she gets lightheaded from lack of air, but Satrasi—ever attuned to her—notices before she does. He pulls away, and she can't help the panting whine she lets out at even that minuscule separation. With an echoing groan, he keeps his lips on her skin, like he can't stop tasting her.

Quicker than she expects, his hot breath is against her ear once again, while his hand moves to cup her ass, adjusting her against him until she feels firm evidence of his desire right where she needs it.

"What do you *want*, little bite?"

Her hips automatically buck, a clear invitation for more, but she answers aloud so there's no ambiguity. "You. I want *you*."

Chapter Eight

"That can be arranged." Satrasi captures Rella's lips in an open-mouthed kiss, ravenous and consuming.

She does her best to hang on for the ride. However, she's not as caught off guard this time, so she slides her tongue along his, pressing into the kiss to flick the tip against his teeth in a daring, hungry move of her own. When he groans, Rella pushes her advantage, anchoring her hands in his clothes to pull herself up, to better angle the kiss so she can taste more of him, so she can lick the brine straight from the source.

"Greedy girl," Satrasi says, lips brushing hers. "How have you kept this appetite from me? How long have you wanted this?"

Rella blinks lazily up at him. How long? When? What silly questions. Although... 'always' isn't quite right. He's always been fascinating and beautiful and captivating. Was there a specific moment when she realized it was more? When it became about more than aesthetic appearances and loyalty and trust, when he solidified in her mind, body, and soul.

It was... It was, *of course*, she wants Satrasi—all of him, in every way she can have him, of course. It wasn't a decision or something she dwells on. She can't remember the moment that must exist, when she went from finding him interesting to look at to aching down to her fingertips to touch him. From finding him a fine admiral to serve under to the only one she ever would. From appreciating to hungry. But at some point, it made sense. It was obvious.

Who wouldn't want him? Wouldn't want to touch him? Wouldn't want to be touched in return? Who else could compare? Who could she want more than her admiral? *Of course.*

She arches her back in reply, pressing her lips against his still-open mouth and giving up on trying to pinpoint the moment he's asking for. "Don't know." Does it even matter when they're finally here? "Longer than I didn't," she settles on. Although, if he insists on discussing this... She pulls away enough to look at him under her lashes, courage racing through her veins as she asks, "What about you?"

His hand slides up into the small of her back, keeping her against him. "Far, far longer than I didn't," he replies, pressing a kiss to her lips. His hair tentacles weave lightly into her own hair. "You've always been so striking, so unique. Like no one I've ever met."

She shakes her head, and he strengthens his grip to stop the movement.

A falsely stern look appears on his face as he disputes her disbelief that *he* could think such a thing about *her.* "Yes, you have." He tilts his head to the side. "You've truly not known you've had me on the hook?"

Her mouth wets at the very idea she might have had his attention for so long, so securely. She gives him an open-mouthed kiss, tongue seeking his. If she can have him, she wants him.

Now.

Vexingly, he pulls away from her chase with a smirk before narrowing his eyes. "You've acted as though you've known. That was why I didn't push. I thought you didn't want me."

Rella shakes her head, mind spinning from his words far more than his kisses. "I've known you'd support me since you first asked me to join you. I knew that you trusted me after the carrier victory message," Rella says, trying to adjust to such a fundamental shift in her worldview. "But I never presumed there was anything more than what we had. That you'd be interested in *me*."

He chuckles. There's an edge to the sound that causes adrenaline to jolt through her bloodstream. Satrasi always makes her feel so gloriously alive.

"Oh, my little messenger, the things I've thought about you." His forehead touches hers as he breathes his words into her mouth. "The things I've wanted from you. The things I still want."

"Yeah?" Rella asks breathlessly, core clenching at the suggestion in his words and the deep timbre of his voice. Her fingers tighten where they hold Satrasi, her strength tiny compared to his, but it seems to be enough in this wild, unreal moment. "Like what?" She licks her lips, thirsty for him—for his words.

"So many things. I always want you by my side. But right now," he says, eyes darkening as he presses a brief kiss to her lips, "I want you in my bed." Satrasi trails more kisses along her jawline. "Want to keep you there for days."

She moans at the thought; she would like nothing more than that. The room has already gone foggy at the edges, inconsequential and indistinct from the sharp reality that is Satrasi in her arms.

He nibbles at her ear. "I want you to forget the rest of the world exists." His voice is gravelly by now and heavy with desire. "Everything except for you and me."

Satrasi pushes her down onto the table, her ass thumping the top as he fills her vision. He stays far enough back that his eyes bore into hers. "Want you right here, right now." All four eyes go half-lidded as he takes her in: her heaving chest, the heat in her cheeks, the needy look in her eyes that she can nearly see reflected in his own dark, dilated pupils. "Is that what you want?"

She thinks he already knows the answer, but she's not surprised he wants to hear it, the same way her head is spinning with *his* words. "Yes, yes." Her words nearly trip over each other, the most inarticulate she's been in ages. "That's *all* I want."

He smirks, hands tightening on her. "Then we are in agreement."

He reaches for one of the communication lines she forgot was even there, pressing a button. His eyes don't leave hers even as low static crackles through the room. "Elliot? I am not to be disturbed for the rest of the day at least, unless the fleet is aflame. Every. Single. Ship. Is that clear?"

He doesn't wait for the response to come through; his hand is back on her, his mouth too, consuming her thoughts. So occupied is she with his mouth that his clever fingers catch her by surprise when the last button on her waistcoat comes undone. He peels it off her, and she helps him. Her hands don't return to clutching at him—no, it's time for her to begin removing his clothes. He already has a head start on hers.

He chuckles when her intentions become clear, shrugging out of his already unbuttoned overcoat with ease, but choosing instead to distract her from his more difficult waistcoat. "Gonna leave marks all over you," he says huskily.

"Oh, yes." The words escape from her lips, heavy with want.

He flashes a grin before his teeth sink into the join of her neck and shoulder. Not hard enough to break the skin, but hard enough that she gasps. Then he sucks on that very spot, and Rella can't help the moan the sensation pulls from her.

The thought that there'll be physical evidence of Satrasi's touch, that he wants there to be, sends her spiraling higher.

"Like that, do you?"

"More, please…" Rella's breath catches on a whine.

He doesn't wait for more of an answer and his hand cups her breast through her thin linen shirt. She stutters out something resembling his name, fingers once more clutching at his clothing rather than actively removing it. But how is she supposed to think when he's trying so hard to make her come undone? The sensations his mouth and hands are invoking threaten to overwhelm her. Her mind is hazy; why wouldn't she want to drown in his touch?

Satrasi's progress along her collarbone is evidenced by the pulsating spots now deprived of the lips and teeth that formed them—a trail of marks left in his wake she hopes take a long, long time to fade. She can't tell if the sole purpose of his hand on her chest is to send zaps of pleasure directly to her core, but if it is, it's certainly working. He tweaks a nipple with the barest hint of his claws coming out to play, and Rella groans at the sharp sensation.

She tears at her linen shirt, wanting that sensation of skin against skin. Rella doesn't care when the flimsy fabric rips; she wants more. More of Satrasi. More of this moment.

A nudge at her hips, in addition to the hand on her chest and the hand approaching the close of her trousers, causes her eyes to dart down. Sure enough, while his hands are otherwise occupied, his tentacles are braced on each side of her, holding her in place for him to touch as he sees fit. Heat scorches through Rella because she wants as much of Satrasi touching her as possible, wants to feel him against—

Her thoughts cut off with a cry when his mouth gets low enough to envelop a peaked nipple, her shirt finally pulled back enough to allow him unfettered access. His mouth is cool against the skin of her chest, his teeth prickling as his tongue laps at her nipple.

Nothing could pull her mind away from those overwhelming feelings except the buttons on her split-skirt trousers giving way. His large hand cups between her legs, and she throws her head back with a cry at all that lovely pressure and friction exactly where she so desperately needs it. One of her hands grips tightly at the back of his neck, and since multiple of his hair tentacles wrap around her wrist, he doesn't mind as he growls in triumph.

As he grinds the palm of his hand against her, fingers pressing teasingly along her slit, he groans so loudly that it nearly drowns out her own moan. "So *wet* for me."

Without waiting, he glides two fingers through said wetness. Impatiently, she bucks her hips so they finally slide inside her. Her nails dig into his skin as she tries to ride through the incredibly full sensation of finally having him inside her. Even though his fingers are thick, she's slick enough that he easily slides another into her heat. He pumps them in and out, panting and groaning against her neck.

Rella's still wearing the torn remains of her shirt, but his tentacles pull her trousers off before returning to their places tight on her hips.

She still feels so hot and she's only whirling higher. The steady rhythm he's established is satisfying, but it's not enough. He's too in control, having halted nearly all his movements to focus on his fingers stroking just right inside her, and she doesn't want that. She wants *Satrasi*: surrounding her, pressing against her, taking everything he wants, everything she's offering... consuming her.

Out of control, for her.

"*Harder*," she pleads, nearly unable to recognize her own strained and desperate voice as it reaches her ears. "Won't break, *please*."

Not only is his next thrust harder, but he curls his fingers on the way out.

She whines, inner walls convulsing around him, suddenly on the precipice of climax.

"I know what you need," he growls, hand back to massaging her breast, teeth back at her neck. "I know just how to fuck you, my little bite," he promises.

Rella's strung so tight as he puts everything he has into taking her apart at the seams. His fingers twisting on each thrust, his palm on her clit, his fingers on her nipple, the marks he's etching into her skin. Her hands clench around him as she rides out the sensations, trying to make this last forever. In the end, it's a miracle she manages to last as long as she does before shattering in his hold.

She surfaces from a haze of bliss to find she's curled against his chest and presses a kiss to his neck. When he pulls his fingers from her, she sinks her teeth into his skin in protest at the sudden emptiness.

Satrasi chuckles darkly. His fingers stroke tauntingly along her slit, making her hips jerk. Then he takes a step back, as if he thinks she might need space.

Luckily, Rella's mind is so overwhelmed with lust that she's able to take advantage of the opportunity he's presented. She follows him, sliding off the counter in his wake and right down to her knees.

Satrasi makes a strangled sound as her hands undo the catch of his trousers, glad she'd managed to get his belt off earlier.

Single-minded in her determination, her small hand reaches in as soon as she's parted the cloth of his pants.

"Yes..." His own hand lands on her head, encouraging her, as she wraps her hand around his cock.

It's the same deep blue as the rest of his skin, only getting darker at the tip, which is covered in red nodes that begin midway down his shaft cluster at the head. He's slick too—she can feel it when she strokes him from tip to root, easing her movements, helping wipe *his* mind of anything that isn't her touch.

Turnabout has never been so satisfying.

She slides her hand back down and loosely twists her palm against his tip, feeling his textured head. More pre-cum spills for *her*. He moans, the sound enhanced by the way the maw in his chest breaks open to growl simultaneously. The combined sound sends shivers down her spine and renewed heat between her legs. She flicks her gaze up along his glorious body, at the way his head is thrown back, hair tentacles reaching wildly for something that isn't there, chest heaving, before her eyes fix back on the prize in her hand. Rella strokes him again, eyes tracking a particular bead of blue-white pre-cum. She needs to know what Satrasi tastes like.

"Rella!" He practically roars her name when, with no preamble, she licks his head. "Oh gods, *more.*" She doesn't need any further persuasion and then takes several inches of his cock into the warm cavern of her mouth. A distant thud suggests his tentacles have hit the wall in surprise. His grip on her head tightens, hand weaving into her hair as he holds her still, claws pricking her scalp delightfully.

Satrasi tastes salty, but not overwhelmingly so, just enough to make her thirsty for more. Rella flicks her tongue and swallows, humming as she appreciates how satisfying it is to have him filling her mouth. His cock twitches in the heat of her mouth. She looks up languidly at the sharp sound of a *crack.*

Satrasi's hand, the one not on her head, must have been clutching the edge of the counter; that wood is now broken off in his fingers. His hair is tying itself in knots, twisting and untwisting, while his tentacles have wrapped around the metal support beam overhead as if they need to hang onto something solid.

Emboldened by the clear loss of control she's managed to inspire, she tries to take more of him into her mouth, but his hand holds her in place.

"Fuck, your *mouth,*" he growls as he shuts all of his eyes tight.

She hums in agreement before fluttering her tongue along his length. His hand spasms, and she's able to bob forward this time, determined to take as much of him as possible. She's grateful to have befriended those brothel workers when Satrasi hits the back of her throat and *whines*.

Rella has never felt more powerful or more fortunate than in this moment. Satrasi is at her mercy. Hers to pleasure.

She keeps one hand at his base while the other braces on his hip. She begins to move, up and down his length, because this isn't everything she wants. She needs him to lose his control, lose his mind, spill down her throat. She needs to unwind him as thoroughly as he unwound her.

Rella's able to find a rhythm, breathing around him, but Satrasi's regained some of his control. His hand rests on her head, and there's no strain against the hand she has on his hip. There's less of those noises she's craving. He's thick and finally warming up in her mouth, twitching slightly with each stroke of her hand, but it's not right—it's too comfortable. She wants him as desperate as she was.

"That's it," Satrasi croaks, his voice like gravel, and pride thrum through her. The fingers in her hair tighten when she swallows around him before he reins himself in again. He keeps having to regain that control, over and over again, little pulsing movements against her head. She wants him to lose even that bit of composure.

"Won't break, little bite."

She pictures his smirk, his dark eyes, as he parrots her own words back at her. Without thought she lets her teeth lightly scrape along his length the next time she takes him in.

His fingers spasm and tighten, holding her in place, as he growls, loud and feral. "*Fuck.*"

She moans around him and he shudders. Hollowing her cheeks, fluttering her tongue against the textured head of his cock at the top of her stroke, makes his hips buck forward erratically as he moans. Triumph fills her as she employs every trick she knows: tongue against his head, pressing him against the roof of her mouth, and stroking relentlessly. A glance up reveals he's finally lost in the act, eyes hazy as her own, until he lets out a growl of warning.

Rella looks directly into his red and black eyes and swallows around him deliberately, her hand tight on his ass to keep him where he needs to be.

His breathing is ragged, chest heaving, the tongue from his second mouth lolling as he strains against her.

Heat races through her veins in anticipation of him coming undone. She rubs her thighs together, whimpering around him in need of friction only he can provide, and sucks him down again.

A loud groan of metal from somewhere above is followed by her name on his lips and his hand holding her tight against him by the hair, Satrasi floods her mouth with his cum. There's more than she expects, giving credence to that particular rumor about demons—she wonders if the others are true too. Rella swallows hastily, the additional pressure making his moan pitch higher. He tastes more acidic than she expected. She finds herself quickly addicted, trying to not let any leak out even as she softens her mouth around him.

When a flick of her tongue against his head stabs a noise from him that shivers through her, she pulls off entirely. Panting and lightheaded, she leans back and spots the now-bent metal beam his tentacles hang limply from. She wipes around her mouth, catching anything she missed, and licks her fingers clean with a pleased hum even as she pulls in desperately needed air.

A growl from deep in Satrasi's chest makes her look at him. His eyes are fixated on her mouth, her fingers—his cum.

Rella purposely slides two fingers past her swollen lips and envelops them completely to clean them off.

Satrasi bares his teeth at her, an open-mouthed snarl on his lips. His hands close on her upper arms—tight enough to bruise later, she thinks with giddy hope. His tentacles close around her hips and under her ass as he hauls her up. He slants his lips over hers hard and licks into her mouth. His teeth nip at her, an unending growl thrumming through them both.

Using skilled hands and tentacles, he does a thorough job of getting both of them completely naked without letting up on the kiss. Rella's dizzy from lack of air as well as the all-consuming nature of his hunger. Satrasi's hands run up and down her sides, caressing everywhere in his quest to paint his claim over every inch of her skin.

It's not until he pulls back to look at her that he falters from his single-minded quest. One of his hands goes to her hip, likely to angle her best, only to freeze a hair's breadth before he touches skin. "What is this?" Satrasi demands, true surprise in his voice even though he must know the answer.

"A tattoo," Rella replies, chest heaving. She looks up at him from beneath her lashes. "Do you not like it?"

It's of his insignia, but whereas the one on his flag is stylized and simplified, the one on her hip is extremely detailed and very obviously *him*. It's still a skull with his hair tentacles, but the eyes, the teeth, the cheekbones, the fact that it's a dark, rich blue with red and black for the eyes...

It's more than the Demon Admiral's flag: it's Satrasi.

"Fuck," he growls, his finger lightly tracing the edge of the design. "When did you even get this? When did you mark yourself like this? Did you... for me?"

"A year ago," she confesses. "It took some time to find a talented enough artist."

Plenty of pirates get tattoos; Satrasi, for one, has black and white angular geometric shapes all over his arms and chest. Plenty of pirates even get tattoos of their flags—but it's on their arms, their chests, places they can show them off. Show what ship, what crew they're with. It's loyalty and bravado and proof of belonging to a group, a signal they aren't alone. That anyone who comes for them is coming after far more. It's a sign they're not going to try to melt back into normal society and leave this life behind. That they can't because it's made its mark on them.

This tattoo on her hip, where so few can see it: that says something completely different. This is private and personal as well as permanent. It's for her. She likes the reminder of how her life has changed, of who the primary architect of that change is—besides herself.

And yes, it's also for him. She's dreamed of his reaction to seeing how she's marked herself as his, wondered at what it might be, hoped her meaning will be clear.

Satrasi's fingers do another circuit of the tattoo before his hand covers the mark—his mark—so beautifully etched on her skin and tugs her close, spreading her legs and planting himself firmly between them. He's hard again as he pushes against her.

It's the first time she can feel his cock where she needs it most, where she's soaked and aching and empty. Her pulse flutters with desire.

"Mine," he proclaims and takes her mouth in a fierce kiss that blissfully wipes away everything else.

Satrasi doesn't stay there long, trekking back down her neck to worry at the marks he's already made, teeth in her flesh, as he rubs against her. The claws of the hand covering her tattoo dig into her ass, and Rella hopes they leave a mark too.

Her hand trails down his chest and along the edges of his secondary mouth. The tongue that licks her hand is large and rough; her mind races with how it might feel against the rest of her as she pets it like she did his cock.

"I need to be inside you, *now*," he demands, voice jagged and abyssal, almost unrecognizable as the calm, confident admiral.

It's the best thing she's ever heard, the best thing to ever know: that it's all because of her.

"*Yes*, I need you so *bad*. Please, please, please, Satra-asi." Her voice breaks on his name as he pushes his thick cock into her. Rella's so wet—and so is he—that he slides smoothly in, only his size slowing him down at all. She clenches around him as he fills her up and leaves her aching in an entirely different, better way.

Her hands scrabble at his shoulders when he starts to pull out before she's used to the feeling of him inside. A high-pitched whimper escapes her when he thrusts even deeper a second later. The feral growl that leaves both of Satrasi's mouths makes her feral herself as she tightens her grip, wraps her legs around him, and clenches her heat around his cock, needing to keep him inside her for longer before she can even think of letting him move again.

Distantly, she hears her own voice. Whatever she manages to garble out must make enough sense to him, because he obliges her, keeping his hard cock buried deep for the moment. She has no chance to try to gather her scattered thoughts as his mouth is on her neck, sucking kisses where bruises were just a few hours ago. His tentacle in the arch of her back presses her close to his chest; that second tongue licks over her breast, rough on her nipple. It all encourages her to push even closer, makes her feel voracious. All she wants is *more*, all she can think is *more* as she squirms eagerly closer.

"More," Rella pants, hips jerking and grinding against him. She's not sure when she switched from wanting stillness to needing friction, but she has. "Please, I need you to move now, please!"

As soon as the words leave her lips, Satrasi thrusts into her with a swear of his own. His skin ripples as his muscles flex, all of his powerful body focused and working only in bringing them both pleasure.

The buds on his cock rub against her inner walls in the best way possible. Rella trembles and keens as Satrasi hits somewhere deep inside her no one else has ever reached. Every muscle in her core clenches from the intensity of the pleasure shooting through her veins.

A tentacle keeps her leg in place so his hand can flick the nipple his tongue isn't occupied with. She tries desperately to hold on and help meet Satrasi's powerful thrusts with her own. Then his tentacle presses against her clit as he strokes in, and she crashes over the edge with a piercing cry, tightening and tugging on his hair tentacles as she convulses around him.

His moan reverberates through her, extending the waves of heat and satisfaction flooding her body. Then he swells and comes with a cry, flooding her core.

Her hips jerk as Satrasi fucks her through both of their aftershocks before finally stilling, slumping over her. Slowly, slowly, her breathing eases, as does Satrasi's, but neither of them let go. No. That won't be happening anytime soon, not if she has anything to say about it.

Carefully, he gathers her in his arms, and she whimpers at the way the movement jostles him inside her. He switches their positions, sitting himself down on the counter and adjusting Rella so she's straddling his lap, leaning against his chest.

His lower tongue licks her lightly, just enough to make goosebumps ripple across her skin before that mouth closes. His tentacles stay around her waist and her hips while his hands smooth down her back.

She returns to tracing patterns on his skin, contentment lapping through her as she lets the reality of what has finally happened sink in.

Nuzzling against him, she presses an open-mouthed kiss to his throat and murmurs, "*Mine,*" into his shoulder.

With a hum, he tilts her chin up to kiss her. "Yours."

Like embers coming to life, heat curls through her. Unhurried kisses slowly intensify as she kneels up, hands cradling his face even as she whines when his cock slips out of her.

Rella loses track of time until eventually Satrasi pulls back, eyes dark and half-lidded. "Need a bed for what else I have planned for you."

She smiles lazily. "Yeah?"

Rella tangles her hands in his hair tentacles; they wrap around her hand and wrist while her other arm loops more securely around his neck. He takes the move as the implicit agreement it is, sliding his hands down to her ass and standing up with her secured to him. His hold is firm and possessive, and she luxuriates in it.

He doesn't bother picking up any of the clothes scattered about the room as he carries her to the door to his personal quarters. Pressing her against it, he uses the claws on one hand to undo the lock, his mouth back to worrying the marks he's already left all over her.

When the lock clicks, Satrasi pulls away, and Rella stays propped against the door, letting him look his fill because it means she gets to do the same.

He leans down to kiss her. "Never going to get enough of you, am I, little bite?"

"No," Rella says with a smile and a shake of her head, finally secure in that knowledge, holding it in her heart like the precious gift it is. She pulls herself back into Satrasi's arms to murmur in his ear, "But neither will I."

CHAPTER NINE

BONUS

R ella thought she would be nervous now that the time had come to actually get her tattoo, but she was only excited. It had taken time to save the coin for it, but really it had been the artist she had been waiting on. She needed the right tattooist, one who could do the design she'd taken months to refine justice.

The tattoo was going to take more than one session, of course, with the amount of color Rella wanted, but today was the first step and she was eager. She had been careful not to show that when haggling over the work, not wanting the price to go up any higher than it was. Paying fair was fine, and she wanted the work to be worth it, but she had no interest in paying a half-penny more than that.

There weren't any other customers in the shop when she walked in. Rella had agreed to an early morning time and the majority of Tilly's customers were still sleeping off the night's festivities.

"Good morn," Tilly herself greeted Rella, looking up from where she was organizing supplies. The older woman had run this shop for over a decade. Her easy movements spoke to her comfort and experience.

"Good morn," Rella replied, blinking as she tried to adjust her eyes from the bright morning sun to the interior of the shop.

"I'll still be setting everything right for ye while my apprentices wake to join," Tilly explained, gesturing both to the myriad of bottles and implements in front of her as well as upstairs where said apprentices must sleep. "So wander the shop as ye please. It's best to stay on yer feet until it's time to stick ye. Ye'll be sittin' long enough as I work as it is."

Rella nodded. "Understood."

A display of previous tattoo work Tilly or the others in her shop must had inked were arrayed on the wall to her right. There was a wide variety in images and words, not all in the language Rella spoke, but the through-line was color. Vivid roses and hearts bloomed bright red, with green stems and leaves. Bleached white bones and yellow poison dripped from skulls she recognized from other pirate insignias. Royal purple and deep, deep blue highlight a handful of noble crests, making it clear people from all walks knew where to come for this quality work.

By the time Rella had done a leisurely circle of the shop to end up where Tilly was fussing, two apprentices had joined her. Only one looked young, but both followed Tilly's instructions to the letter despite the yawns they exchanged. The counter was set to exacting precision, a mix between an apothecary's array of potions and a physician's tray of implements, with a dyer's row of colors.

"We're about ready for ye," Tilly said. "If ye gotta piss, now's the time, 'cause I don't stop once I start."

Rella wisely took Tilly up on her offer, and they were all set to start by the time she was back from relieving herself.

Before she could lay down, Tilly stopped her with an outstretched hand. "Payment first," Tilly's voice brokered no nonsense. "This'll be three sessions and you'll pay each in full before I put needle to skin."

Rella and her had already haggled out price and timing, but she wasn't surprised at Tilly's insistence.

"Here," Rella dropped a pouch with the requisite amount of silver into Tilly's hand. Rella had brought exactly enough for this work and not a coin more beyond the copper she'd spent on breakfast walking over here. Oftentimes, depending on the skill of the tattooist, one could be left groggy from the numbing agent and she'd no desire to get jumped for all she had before someone noticed who's crew she was on.

Tilly's motioned for Rella to lay down while she counted the coins. The younger apprentice, a girl younger than Rella had been when she joined Satrasi's crew, directed her to remove her loose shirt. Clad in only her breastband, Rella scooches her skirt down, worn specifically for this occasion, to bare her hip for the tattoo.

"I don't care how tedious ye find my process, it don't change for any-one," Tilly said, coin and pouch having disappeared. "There's no changing yer mind with one of mine so yer gonna need to be damn sure, 'cause yer coin's mine now, ye hear?"

"I hear ye," Rella replied.

Tilly gave a decisive nod and said to the younger apprentice, "Mark out accordin' to the sketch and be quick about it."

The girl already had charcoal in her hands and, with a glance at Rella's design, began to do as she was bid.

"This is to make sure you like the size you decided on," she told Rella. "Lots of people seem to not expect what they asked for."

It was an odd angle. Staying still and craning her neck didn't work well together, so Rella gave up after a second or so. The older apprentice helpfully slid a wooden crate with some cloth folded on top to help prop up her head. Charcoal on skin was an odd feeling and Rella was glad she wasn't particularly ticklish.

"Done," the young apprentice said a few minutes later.

"Good work, Deli," Tilly said. "Take a look yerself now."

Between angling her neck and the mirror the older apprentice held up for her, Rella could get a good feel for the size. The skull itself was only a vague outline with lines coming off for the tentacles, but it was about the size of her palm, which meant Satrasi would be able to cover even the tentacles with his own palm. Not that she had high hopes for him to actually get the chance to appreciate it, but the imagining was enough. So was the mirror's reflection of the outlines of Satrasi's mark on her.

She had scars from fights since she joined Satrasi's crew, and most of what she owned was all from this life, but she wanted something permanent and pretty and tied to Satrasi himself. Once she stumbled on the idea of a tattoo, it'd not left her alone.

"Yes."

Tilly grunted and motioned for Rella to lay back down. "Good. Today we'll do the black outline, next time the blue, and last session the red. Vinc here is going to ensure yer not in pain, and that's not out of the kindness of my heart: it's so yer not squirming around while I'm inking. He'll also be sealing everything at the end. Proprietary formula with rare ingredients from out in the Unbroken, but yer already be knowin' that. It's why you seafolk come to me, isn't that right?"

"That, and the color," Rella acknowledged. Wear and tear on sailors, especially pirates, was intense, and she had no desire to come back in a few years to get inked all over again with potentially a new artist. She wanted it done once and done right.

"Color's got secrets, too. Some mundane and others from the Unbroken," was all Tilly would say. Purist shops refused to use any demonic or even 'exotic' ingredients in their work, but Rella thought that was foolish. There were limits to what ordinary ingredients could do and as long as the shop had the right reputation for it, picking one that took advantage of all the available techniques was just a better choice. Ordinary tattoos faded with time, resourceful shops knew how to prevent that from happening all together. Not to mention the other capabilities it gave them, like vibrant color in Tilly's case. "While color might be why yer here, this black is the most important. It'll take the longest too and I'll not be stopping once I start. So... hold still."

"Yes, ma'am," Rella replied, with all the respect a master at their craft was owed in her voice.

Vinc started to work first, with a pinch to her side as he set about numbing the area for the tattoo. Rella knew that plenty don't bother, and some were just as liable to kill you with the special blend of demonic poison they use, but the numbing was crucial for speed. That was why she had been so careful when selecting this shop.

Sooner than she expected, Tilly was pulling up her chair to begin, while Vinc and Deli hovered nearby to assist. Tilly had nothing more to say except to bark orders, intense in her focus as she put the first needle to skin. Vinc's work was good: Rella can't feel a thing.

While Tilly might be content to stay silent, the apprentices still talked. Vinc was mostly teaching Deli, but she managed to draw him into idle conversation more often than not. Still, it wasn't long until a lull in their work led her to set her sights on Rella.

"Who do you ship out with?" Deli asked. Rella saw Vinc give her a look, but Deli pouted. "I only just moved here, you can't blame me for not knowing every flag for every ship yet."

"If there's any you ought to know," Vinc gave Rella an almost apologetic glance, "it's this one, girly."

"Then tell me," Deli said crossly, handing over a fresh little bottle of black ink to Tilly without the tattooist needing to say a word. She met Rella's eyes. "Please."

"Admiral Satrasi," Rella said, pride evident in her voice. "His personal ship."

"Truly?" Deli looked properly impressed, which shouldn't be as gratifying as it was. "We've done some of his other ships but not the Crimson Shadow."

"First time for everything," Vinc said, exasperated. "Stop letting folks know yer as green as ye are."

Deli ignored him to keep staring at Rella with new wonder. "The Demon Admiral himself, wow. Have you met him?"

Rella stifled the urge to laugh. "Yeah, being part of his crew lends to that."

"Have you seen him fight? I hear he's got ten tentacles, black as night, each longer than the tallest man."

"I have seen him fight," Rella said, able to tell this girl wasn't looking for gritty details of life at sea or as a pirate. She was too caught up in the romance of it all. Rella did love hearing the rumors that spread about Satrasi. "But he's not got nearly so many as all that, and the blades he wields in his hands are more than enough to make most folks regret making the mistake of coming at him."

"I heard he bites the heads off of his enemies with his demon mouth," Deli offered up eagerly.

"Skulls are liable to give even the Admiral a stomachache," Rella replied with a shake of her head. She didn't bother to mention that he didn't make a habit of going around without his shirt on to be able to do so, primarily because she wouldn't mind if he did. "So that's not his usual preference."

"But could he?"

Rella started to shrug before remembering she was to keep still. "Probably."

"Wow," Deli breathed, even Vinc looked interested despite himself. Only Tilly didn't give any indication she could hear the talk going on around her.

Deli threw out more rumors that Rella answered with good humor. No, Satrasi wasn't eight feet tall. No, he wasn't a thousand years old. He had only four eyes. Of course he didn't subsist entirely on the blood of his enemies. His claws could grow, but not to the length of a man's forearm.

"So, I'm guessing that having demonic sharks circle his ships to feed mutineers to is also a tall tale?" Vinc said as he refilled the ink vials nearby.

"They're not sharks, not anymore than demons are human."

Vinc paled as he realized there must be some truth to what he said.

Rella smiled as she continued, "And not all his ships, just whichever ship he's aboard. That's what the 'Crimson Shadow' refers to. Water gets real dark red when they feed."

"Is it true that all his crew on board are also all demons?" Deli asked.

"Crew's a mix, humans and demons," Rella replied. "Can't be all demons if I'm one, yeah?"

"Oh, right," Deli acknowledged with a flush. "You just don't seem like a pirate."

"That so?" Rella raised an eyebrow, amused.

"Meaning no disrespect, ma'am," Vinc cut in as he stomped on Deli's foot and ignored the yelp she gave in response.

"None taken," Rella replied. She knew what she looked like off duty and part of that serves her role, so she didn't work hard to correct it. "I get further as a messenger if some folks don't know who I'm carrying word from. Don't need as much muscle to be fast, and the strength I need all comes from here." Rella patted the demon blade hung on her neck instead of strapped to her hip, where it usually was, mindful of the work being done.

"That why ye got demon blood on ye?" Vinc asked.

Since he was in charge of the sealant, Rella wasn't surprised he'd made that connection. She was getting the tattoo sealed with Satrasi's own blood, another option human shops couldn't always offer. Not only did supplying the blood herself cut down on the cost of having to pay for it, but it felt right, since it was his mark she was having sealed. Demon blood had far reaching uses, like keeping a demon blade sharp. In this case, it also could make a tattoo impervious to fading.

"Yeah."

"Lotta trust, letting you keep a vial," he observed, seemingly idly.

Rella's gaze sharpened on him. She didn't appreciate the implication that he didn't believe Satrasi gave it over to her. "Can't bring his words where he isn't and bring it back again if he don't trust me. Wouldn't have gotten a blade if he didn't. And I've had this one for years."

It was a warning, and at least Vinc was no idiot. He backed off.

"'Course, everyone knows his Marlins earn their blades."

Rella let her eyes linger on him before she deliberately dismissed him. "They're one and the same: only Marlin's gotta 'em and ye can't get 'em if yer not a Marlin."

"Right, right."

He decided to head over to the other table to fetch some fresh water. Even Deli wisely kept her mouth shut. There was only the sound of glass and metal clinking as Tilly worked. It was easy for Rella to let her mind drift, speculating over where her next mission would take her, and plotting routes to the most likely targets.

A pat on her leg pulled Rella out the meditative state she was in. Deli helped Rella to her feet, her hip starting to dully ache, but she hadn't lost any balance. Vinc was holding up a mirror again and Rella's spellbound by the dark, thick outline of Satrasi's insignia, the skull with four eyes positioned perfectly to mimic Satrasi's own. The top of the mouth had his teeth, sharp and hungry. The expression on it, the detail to the tattoo: it was everything she wanted and more.

If she got it filled in black or even white like the flag, it would still be a beautiful representation of her life since she joined the Demon Admiral's crew. But she wanted it—no, needed it—to be Satrasi.

"When can I come back for the color?"

The blue was added a month after the first session, personally mixed by another of Tilly's apprentices, with Rella's input for accuracy. That inking took nearly as long as the first and stung more after the fact. Rella had to wait another two months this time to come back for the final addition of the red for his eyes and some white for his teeth.

The most painful part was the demonic sealant. Mixed with an exacting amount of Satrasi's blood, it had to be applied after the numbing agent wore off. Whatever demonic magic it held within the particular combination felt like it burned, although Tillty swore it only felt like it did. Rella hadn't even been allowed to see the result as Tilly had quickly bandaged it up. Rella had been told to wait three weeks to unwrap it and only come back if she was dissatisfied. The look in Tilly's eye told her that never happened, which helped reassure her.

Three weeks later, Rella laden with both nerves and anticipation. Carefully, Rella unwound the bandage from around her and peeled the linen underneath away.

Her breath caught in her throat when she finally saw the tattoo in all its glory. The tentacles looked even more lifelike than after the first session, as though they might start to move at any moment. The look in his eyes was intense and fierce. All the other details of the face from the cheekbones to even the nose hole both matched the flag design and Satrasi himself.

It was perfect.

Rella slowly surfaces from the waters of sleep to the feeling of warm safety. She hums as she wakes, pushing her face into what has to be her pillow on the carrier. There's nowhere else she feels so comfortable, except of course wherever Satrasi is.

All at once, pressure on her hips and the presence she can feel around her slot into place as well. She blinks open her eyes and looks down into Satrasi's four red eyes. A smile spreads across her face reflexively.

"Morning," she says, voice rough from sleep.

He's situated down near her legs, as if he'd started to crawl into bed with her and simply didn't get very far. Both of his large hands are splayed over her skin, one on her bare back where her loose sleep shirt has rucked up and the other high on her thigh. Satrasi presses a kiss to the skin closest to his mouth.

"Good morning, Rella."

"When did you get back?" she asks, reaching a hand out from under the sheet to tangle in his hair tentacles. They are as eager to wrap around her fingers as ever.

"Last night," he murmurs, as quiet as she is, unwilling to break the calm of the early morning. He strokes his hand over the exposed skin of her hip.

"How is it that near everything wakes you up from a dead sleep in a hurry except for me? Hm?"

Rella presses into his touch without thinking. She yawns, tugging lightly with her hold on his head. She wants to bring him closer to her, so she can greet him properly. "I don't know. Perhaps you should try to make more of an impression."

The heat in his eyes says he knows she's teasing but that he can't help but rise to the challenge. With a growl that's more playful than anyone else would ever hear from him, he surges up her body. Large, strong hands cradle her jaw. Satrasi kisses her deeply, expertly, and Rella melts even further in the bed than she already was. When he grinds against her, she can tell all of him is wide awake, and she moans.

"What more of an impression do you require?"

She laughs against his lips, the sound mostly air. Rella still feels languid so soon after waking, but he's quickly pulling the sleep from her veins with his obvious desire.

"None." Her free hand runs down his arm, cool, smooth skin under her fingertips. No new injuries that she can feel, just hard won muscle. "You know trust is what keeps me asleep, nothing else."

Satrasi leans in to nuzzle at her neck, nipping at skin that's free of marks due to how long they've been apart. The feeling of each mild sting zips along Rella's nerves. Instinctively, she starts to move against him, needing more.

"I know." His fingers trace deliberate patterns against her hip and side.

Rella runs her fingers along his hair tentacles and whines when Satrasi pulls away from her neck with a final press of his lips. Satrasi indulges her with another kiss, stroking the flames of her desire, but he pulls away after a few seconds. He dots kisses down her chest, her stomach until he's back at her hips where he was when she first woke up.

Rella finally notices that he's concentrated on tracing the outline of her tattoo. A shiver goes up her spine at his focus, at the careful way he trails along an inked tentacle. He likes to keep his hand on the tattoo, even over her clothes, but this manner of intense study is more unusual. She likes it. For so long, she thought he'd never see the design and even if he did, she'd not truly dreamed it would be as her lover. His appreciation is gratifying.

"It's exquisite," he murmurs. His adroit tongue flicking out to wet his lips and keeping Rella spellbound as always. "The details and the colors. No fading."

"'Course not," Rella replies, only half focused on the words coming out her mouth. The heat gathering between her legs is stealing more of her attention the longer he stares. "Paid too much for it. She promised it never would."

"She was correct." Satrasi's cool breath fans out over the tattoo and Rella shivers. "It's a work of art." He presses an open-mouthed kiss directly between the eyes, which are based on his own, inked permanently on her skin. He pushes back up, hovering over her to better look at the tattoo. "Mine are not so sophisticated."

Bold white and black lines criss-cross his skin, wind around his biceps, his shoulders, and down his spine. They suit him, angular and bold, but Rella would admit they're not intricate or obvious depictions of anything. Reaching down, she follows a white line with her fingertips from his shoulder to the edge of the maw in his chest. There's no lips on that mouth, just a slit down the center of his chest that looks like a scar until it splits to reveal gray, lustrous, wickedly sharp teeth. And that tongue, black with red streaks like the one the the mouth in his head, but longer and rougher. It slides out even now to hungrily flick against her fingers.

Satrasi pets the artwork on her hip. "Yours on me isn't equal to this."

Rella's heart skips a beat. He'd made an offhand mention that one of his tattoos is for her a few days after seeing her own for him, but they'd been interrupted before she could question him further. Rella knows most of his longest serving crew is represented in some manner on his skin. She had been trying to remember to broach the subject, hungry she was for more details about hers.

"Which is it?"

Satrasi glances up to meet her gaze and she can tell something in her voice has gotten his attention. He smirks. "Did I never tell you, little bite?"

Rella's eyes narrow and she grinds against him in retaliation. "No, you didn't."

Satrasi moans, hands clenching on her hips. He swoops back up to her, catching her lips in a kiss, pushing her down onto her back. Rella gets lost in the press of lips, the slide of tongue, and the heat between them.

Slowly, still sipping from her lips, Satrasi pulls away to lay down beside her on his stomach. Rella makes a noise in the back of her throat, half protest, half curiosity. His larger back tentacles move above to bare the notches of his spine where a series of symbols line his back. His finger draws along one in the center, with unerring accuracy.

Bright white and about the size of her palm, it's a circle with a straight horizontal bar across it. It must be a demonic symbol, but she doesn't know it or recognize it. They're usually more complex. This is simple, fundamental. Rella's fingers ghost over the tattoo.

Satrasi tucks his hand under his head as he relaxes under her touch. "It's demonic," he says, voice rough. "Salt."

Rella thinks that over while she traces the circle with firmer fingers. "Because of what I brought you all those years ago?"

"Yes," he admits with a half shrug from his prone position. "And…"

Rella waits with bated breath, unable to stop touching this permanent mark on his skin for her. Not that she didn't understand or enjoy his attention to her tattoo before. But she feels something like fire lick at her bones as she stares and touches his tattoo for her.

"Sea demons have both the danger of reliance on salt and the advantage of not being weak to it. A vital strength."

Rella knows how much Satrasi values his crew, not just those he commands, but the few she would rank as his personal friends. How highly he weighs loyalty, which is hard to find out here in the Unbroken Sea among the lawless and desperate. She's always admired his attachment in light of the dangerous life they lead.

Thinking back on the Satrasi she found in that pool in that cave all those years ago. What that meant to her and that it might have meant as much to him… She presses a reverent kiss to the center of the mark. "I love it."

He levers himself up and over Rella, one hand on the bed and the other landing back on her tattoo. "As I do yours."

The gentle warmth of the moment quickly boils back to heat as they reignite. After a delightfully lascivious kiss, Satrasi trails deliberate open-mouthed kisses down to her breasts while his tentacles wind around her legs and encourage them to wrap around him.

Instead of near his hips, they guide her legs to cross higher on his back, right over his tattoo. Rella starts to move them further down only for Satrasi's hand on her hip to squeeze a warning to stay where she is.

"Right here," he murmurs before nipping at one of her nipples.

Rella starts to voice a question when the maw on his chest opens and its large tongue licks her slit from bottom to top.

"Yes," she cries out, her core clenching around the idea of how he plans to fill her. His second tongue has a rougher texture than the one currently wrapped around her nipple. It feels delicious against her clit and she grinds against him as best she can. "More."

Satrasi growls, the sound reverberating out of both mouths as he switches breasts to give Rella's neglected nipple some attention. One hand still holds her steady by her hip, the other supporting her lower back off the bed, all positioning her perfectly so his larger tongue can lap at her slit. A deeper groan comes from that mouth while he suckles at her breast with his human mouth.

Rella doesn't know how best to ride out the intense heat pouring through her veins except hold on tight, one hand still tangled deep in his hair tentacles and the other clutching desperately at his shoulder. Just in time, because the tentacles maneuver her legs, spreading her thighs wide enough for that inhuman tongue to slide in.

Rella must moan loud enough to wake everyone on this side of the ship. Strong and lithe, Satrasi's tongue sinks in deeper than his usual tongue, deeper than fingers have ever managed. It feels so good she's going to burst.

Satrasi continues to improve the angle at which he's holding Rella, because, soon enough, part of the tongue that isn't inside her is pressed firmly to her swollen clit.

"Yes," Rella mewls and her hips twitch in Satrasi's firm hold when he starts to withdraw his tongue, only to cry out when he thrusts back in. It's so different from his hard cock, but it feels so good. Her mind's gone blissfully blank of anything that isn't Satrasi. Between his practiced attention to her breasts and his demonic tongue fucking her, she can already feel the way her inner walls are pulsing around him in anticipation of her release.

Satrasi must sense that, because his strokes become faster, deeper, as if he's trying to eat her from the inside out. In the end, it's the rasp of his sharp gray teeth, both sets, on her tender flesh that press, but do not break the skin, that pushes her over the edge with a breathy whine as pleasure rolls through her.

Slowly Rella floats back to the present, to the feeling of Satrasi's smaller, but no less wickedly talented tongue lapping up the mess he made of her. She spreads her legs, now resting on the bed, a little wider. She's grateful his continued attention is careful not to overwhelm her nerves as he helps her wind down from her climax. When eventually Rella blinks her eyes open and looks down, he's staring right back at her.

Satrasi licks his lips, shiny with her essence. Smug. "You always taste so delicious, little bite."

Rella gives a pleased hum in reply, unable to form the words to say anything more coherent, especially not when she's still so hungry for him.

Satrasi must understand, given the way he chuckles. He's told her before how pleased he is when he's reduced his messenger to someone beyond words. After one more deliberate flick of her clit that pulls a whimper from her, he shifts up.

Rella groans when what must be a painfully hard erection grinds down against her. Her lover continues to look immensely satisfied with himself as he positions his cock to enter where she is wet and empty. All of his red eyes glint with hunger, all his teeth seem especially sharp as the early morning light hits them. From his tentacles to his tattoos, Satrasi is everything her small town whispered he was: the most dangerous type of demon, the picture of temptation. And he's delicious every time Rella gives in.

"Need you," she manages.

Satrasi doesn't waste any time pushing into her. No matter how Rella loves his tongue, she loves his cock even more. Something he seems intent on reminding her as he slides home, filling her up beautifully. She clenches around him, wanting to ensure he is reminded the reverse is true as well. The strangled sound from deep in his throat is a worthy reward.

"Rella."

Her name never sounds as good as it does when she's rung it out of him. She slides her hand down from his shoulder, rocking her hips to encourage him to move. "Need—"

He surges within her, cutting off her plea and her fingernails scrape down his back in an attempt to hold on. Satrasi hisses in satisfaction as he begins to fuck her in earnest.

Soon, Rella lets go of his back to brace against the bed. She uses that newfound leverage to meet Satrasi's next thrust with a grunt that's nearly drowned out by his moan.

His tentacles stroke down her sides, his claws prick her skin around the tattoo he's still covering with his hand, and the claws on his other hand dig into the sheets beneath them as they move together. His red eyes blaze down Rella's body as he pants, open-mouthed.

"Fuck," Satrasi groans. "You feel…"

"Yeah?" Rella asks, sounding nearly as out of breath as he does and nearly as eager.

"Hot," he pants on a stroke, "wet," he thrusts to the hilt again, "perfect." He tightens his grip on her. "Mine."

Rella moans as the frenzy in her blood builds in anticipation of her peak. "Yours."

Satrasi bears down harder in response, a building subsonic not-quite-growl, not-quite-hum coming from somewhere deep inside him. She knows that means he's close, that knowledge and the vibration push her over the edge.

"Oh!" Sparks of pleasure dance on her nerves as she tightens around him. "Satrasi!"

Rella feels his release as Satrasi shudders, clutching her to him as he comes apart for her. He lands on his side next to her and when he falls onto his back, she goes with him. Together, they succumb to well earned sleep.

Acknowledgements

I want to thank my online followers for being so encouraging and willing to follow me wherever my writing decides to take me. Without your support and comments, I would not be publishing at all, certainly not this novella. You gave me the confidence to finish this original work and publish it.

Thank you also to my lovely beta readers: Sam (the other monster lover in the office) and Lizzy (who's put up with my stories since middle school). You're both so wonderful and I appreciated your help so much!

About the Author

J. A. Lenay has been writing fantastical stories in her head for as long as she can remember and in notebooks since middle school. She finds nothing as motivating to her imagination as her desk job and her commute. She's excited to share her stories with anyone who'll listen. Currently living in the Northeast USA, she fills her days with reading, writing, and time with the people she cares about.

Find J. A. Lenay at:

Tumblr @ jalenay

Website @ jalenay.com

www.ingramcontent.com/pod-product-compliance
Lightning Source LLC
Chambersburg PA
CBHW060440130626
46555CB00005B/2435